Tor books by Andre Norton

Caroline (with Enid Cushing)
The Crystal Gryphon
Dare To Go A-Hunting
Elvenbane*
Flight in Yiktor
Forerunner
Forerunner: The Second Venture
Gryphon's Eyrie (with A. C. Crispin)
Grandmasters' Choice (editor)
Here Aide Monsters
House of Shadows (with Phyllis Miller)
Imperial Lady (with Susan Shwartz)
The Jekyll Legacy (with Robert Bloch)
Moon Called
Moon Mirror
The Prince Commands
Ralestone Luck
Stand and Deliver
Wheel of Stars
Wizards' Worlds
Wraiths of Time

THE WITCH WORLD (editor)
Tales of the Witch World 1
Tales of the Witch World 2
Four from the Witch World
Tales of the Witch World 3

WITCH WORLD: THE TURNING
Storms of Victory

MAGIC IN ITHKAR (editor, with Robert Adams)
Magic in Ithkar 1
Magic in Ithkar 2
Magic in Ithkar 3
Magic in Ithkar 4

*forthcoming

ANDRE NORTON
MOON CALLED

A TOM DOHERTY ASSOCIATES BOOK
NEW YORK

This is a work of fiction. All the characters and events portrayed in this book are fictitious, and any resemblance to real people or events is purely coincidental.

MOON CALLED

A Tor Book
Published by Tom Doherty Associates, Inc.
49 West 24th Street
New York, N.Y. 10010

Cover art by Victoria Poyser
Interior Illustrations by Victoria Poyser

ISBN: 0-812-51533-1

First Tor edition: July 1983

Printed in the United States of America

0 9 8 7 6 5 4

1

Thora lay belly-down in the dew-beaded grass beneath a screen of brush, her attention all for the open meadow beyond—most of all for the weathered building squatting in the middle of that expanse. The cold arose from the earth into her thin, trail-hardened body which, within its covering of weathered leather, melted into the brown-gray of last season's grass and leaves. Patience was a thing she had learned well since last autumn when the Craigs had been overrun by pirates coming upriver from the coast. Those of her people who had survived scattered, to live and die as best they could. She knew that the walls of a determined spirit must stand as strong as a wall of stone when it was a matter of keeping food in one's stomach, to fight the pinch of clawlike hunger. It was that hunger which had drawn her here.

The hour was mid-morning, and, out on the new-showing grass of those open fields, the wild cattle whose trail she had followed had begun to graze. She let fall from her mouth the spittle-gummed cud she had been chewing since dawn—a hunter's trick to chew upon the food which most attracted the game. Now, almost absently, Thora scratched a small hole in the earth to bury that wad. At present it was more important to consider the building.

The structure was very old, perhaps even dating from the Before Time. Yet it seemed to have stood the passing of seasons better than most of the ruins she had chanced upon. Long and low against the ground, it had windows like slits, into which there was no looking from this distance. Beside it were newer pieces of man's handiwork—corrals of poles well set, the earth within them trampled as if there had recently been animals penned there. Yet no smoke rose from the chimney.

Thora edged farther forward. Beside her a darker form stirred and lifted a prick-eared head, turning to meet her own dark blue eyes with two of yellow-gold. The girl lifted her upper lip as might the animal express a noiseless snarl. Her companion rose to four feet, trotted carefully on through the sheltering brush, downslope toward the building. Keen as her own sight and hearing had become, she lacked the sharpness of Kort's senses.

Danger hung about any shelter. Men, though they were now near ten generations from the Before Time, still had an inbred desire to use such, to loot if they could. In her own belt scabbard rested a knife found in just such a place, its blade much thinned by many sharpenings but still better steel than any Craig Smith might beat out of those bits of metal traders brought. That had been her mother's—and from farther back, a handsome heritage from Foremothers now dim in time.

There were no signs that this country had ever been turned by the plow. Instead the only breakage she could trace in the grass cover was a wide path, so well trodden that it remained bare earth. This must be, Thora decided, some traders' way. Not that the shelter might be any more safe because of that. Some traders were rumored to be hardly better than raiders in their treatment of any loner they chanced upon who had anything worth the stealing. Her hand slipped down her body now to assure herself that what she wore about her under her breeches was still safe.

She watched Kort cross the open below, moving with a flash of speed near to the blink of an eye. Until he reached the wider slit that marked the door of the building.

Thora near jerked upright. Her hand went to her knife's hilt. Within that building there was life! Despite that Kort showed no sign of going on guard. She sought to blink out sight, to allow that feeble other sense of hers to come into better focus. Life—man?

No. What she caught was not the emanation of one of her own species. This was very different. There was trouble, however—great hunger—pain— Kort raised his head in a gesture she knew well. Thora flittered forward with hardly more than a slight stirring of the grass through which her hide boots passed. There was life—and there was trouble.

Prudence warned her to slip away, but something would not allow such a retreat. Thora set spear to her thrower and ran on to the corral and along the wall of that to the door where Kort awaited her.

The doorward was closed by a tight barrier, not too long put in place. But from its latch hole the braided thong dangled—a clear sign that this was to be open to any traveler. Thora nodded to Kort. The huge hound closed his jaws upon that string and gave it a jerk, a second pull bringing the door open. Thora edged along to peer within.

There was a whiff of strong odor, strange odor. Her nose wrinkled, as she realized that part of that stench was born of hurt or illness. Whatever was inside must be helpless for she heard no movement. So she ventured into a much-shadowed long room. It took a moment for her sight to adjust to the very dim light for the lower windows were shuttered, and only the narrow cracks under the eaves were free.

A table, some stools were at the chamber's center. There were two doors, one on either side of the fireplace, both closed, while to her right and left the walls had bunks built along them. On one something moved and Thora tensed, spear coming up.

Whatever it was lay or huddled on the bunk farthest from her on the left, in the gloomiest of corners. So she saw only a heaving mound from which came a hissing cry—

Step by careful step Thora advanced. Behind her Kort stood alert, ready, and the girl knew that she need not fear anything coming at her unseen as she explored. So she reached the side of the bunk.

Here that fetid smell was very strong. What or who lay there had gone untended and befouled of body. That hissing had died away. Thora raised her spear, prodded at the bar of the window shutter just above the bunk— sending that thudding onto the next sleeping shelf. Daylight flooded in.

She gasped. What lay there raised a paw—a hand?—feebly into the full light as if begging for help. But what was it? She had never seen nor heard of such a life-form in all her life. No trader's tale of long wandering had suggested that this might exist in the land.

Skeleton thin—was it a child? No, the body was humanoid in shape, but no man nor woman had ever grown such hair, matted and stinking now, along bone-thin limbs, over the whole starved body. The head, which it tried to raise, was round as a great ball of coarse fur. But the thing's face was covered only by a thin down, where it was not so slicked and dried by mucus and a crust of blood to be visible at all.

The eyes were disproportionately large and appeared to have no pupils. Rather they resembled shining stones of deep red, like the heart of a dying fire. Also, though it had hand-like appendages, those possessed long thin digits which were more claws than fingers. The feet were flat and broad, toeless and spurred at the heel.

One of those feet was twisted, the skin broken. A half-open mouth showed cruelly pointed teeth, the canines extra long, protruding over the thin lips. Above was a flat spread of flesh in which were nostrils.

Thora's tongue wet her own lips. The creature was so strange—so utterly unlike an animal. She felt a faint repulsion, until those red eyes met hers and she staggered. Perhaps she even cried out, for she heard Kort's warning growl. Pain—fear—pain—that fed into her. Knife and spear fell from her hands as she clamped her palms over her ears. Though she was not hearing at all—she was sensing it—as if some force pierced her slim, tough body.

Then the lids dropped over the fiery pits of eyes, the thing going limply still. It must have put into that sending the last of fast-failing strength. Thora knew that she could not leave it here to die—whatever it might be. It was alive and her own service for the Lady would not permit her to turn her back upon it.

It possessed intelligence, of that she was certain. Nor was it any threat to her. Had she been led here? Anything was possible when one was Chosen and thus attuned so closely to the Lady.

Speedily she went to work. Sometime later she had a camp in a small wood, well away from the building which she still distrusted. She had moved the creature near to a spring Kort had nosed out. There, with handfuls of damp grass, she sponged the skeleton-thin body free of filth. A small fire of dried sticks which would give off little smoke had been kindled under a tree, the branches would further break any rising smoke. She had left the comatose creature only long enough to make the kill which had drawn her to this meadowland, a season-old calf which fell to her practised throwing spear. Now a battered pot from the house bubbled with water over the fire. Into that she dropped shavings of meat and added pinches of dried herbs which she carried in her backpack.

The foot of her charge had been badly in-jured at the ankle; that she had bound up with what healing care she knew. She had already dribbled into the fanged mouth what water she could induce it to swallow. It was a female, plainly so in spite of the wasting of its body.

That body was as small as a child's. Were they both standing, Thora believed, the bushy head of her charge would hardly reach to her own shoulder. The skin beneath the hair she had washed was dark, but the fur hair itself dried into a silver-gray, darker on the back, the outer sides of the arms—while the head mop was entirely black. Lips were purple, as were the gums from which those teeth sprouted. Between those lay a very long dark tongue, which had shown as she struggled to get it to drink, of the same color. The fingers were indeed claws, shining black as were the heel spurs.

When the broth was done Thora lifted the creature's head against her knees and began the task of getting nourishment into it. But the head continued to turn away, the hands' claws arose feebly to push aside what she had to offer. Then Kort joined her, between his jaws a piece of raw meat, dripping blood, which had been part of his portion of their shared kill. One clawed hand flailed out, caught as if by chance at the meat. Then the creature opened eyes, gave a weak cry, and pulled at what the hound held. Against Thora's attempt to stop it, those claws brought the slopping piece of flesh in its mouth—sucked avidly.

The girl battled down her disgust. It was plain that what was needed was raw meat, and, if that would restore the creature, she was willing to provide such. She sliced off gobbets from the portion she had laid ready for broiling, swiftly discovering from small hisses and motions that what it seemed to want the most were those still bloody. It licked at such avidly.

Finally the furred one lapsed into quiet and Thora settled it back on a nest of grass—drinking the herb-seasoned broth herself as that cooled. She threaded portions of flesh on sticks to broil over the fire and planned on smoking what she could of much of the kill. Kort, his middle distended—for, like all his kind, he ate heavily when the occasion offered—lay on the other side of the fire, his head on his forepaws, at rest but not asleep.

Perhaps Kort found the stranger as puzzling as Thora did. Though he had showed no sign of wariness. She had learned to watch his reaction to any situation, beginning on that morning when he had come between her and her return to Craig House, so saving her from the raiders. She valued his companionship very highly, knowing that she could have sought no better trail companion.

Because Thora was Chosen she had no strong house ties among her own people. When she had been born with the Mother's sign so plainly set between her breasts she had been given the training which would lead in time to her being one of the Three. Weapons were hers and trail knowledge, learning concerning beasts and herbs, and the Ritual. She had not yet taken up the Wand and the Cup, and would not, until Malva the Old died or withdrew to the Upper Heights. Then it would be her turn to be the Maid. Not for her any hearthside or the bearing of a child.

Not that the thought of that troubled Thora at all. Her mind was eager for learning, and she had gone most happily into instruction. She had indeed been in a dream vision during the night the raiders struck. That was what had kept her away from Craig House.

Perhaps there were others who had also gotten away. But she had struck first for the High Shrine, knowing that she must save the sacred things if she had time. Breathlessly she had labored, Kort on watch, putting well-wrapped treasures into the crypt below the Mid-stone. All she had brought with her was the girdle of chain against her skin, its pendant smooth and cool hanging just below her navel—the disc of the silver moon at full, set with a milky gem at which she often gazed longingly (wishing that she had the strength of power for the far-seeing, but for that her training was too little advanced).

The pendant shone clearly against her body now as she stripped off her trail clothing to bathe in the rill which trickled off from the spring, and finished her bath by rubbing herself dry with grass into which she twisted

some of her herbs so that there was a fresh
and pleasant scent to her skin. The clothing
she wiped clean as she could and hung to dry
on bushes, moving back and forth in the dap-
ple of sun and shade as she busied herself with
the preparation of the meat for drying.

Kort raised his head once, pointing nose to
the meadow where they had left the remnants
of the kill. There sounded a squealing and a
growling as the scavengers gathered to this
unexpected bounty.

Thora was very carefully putting a fresh
edge to the blade of her ancient knife when she
became aware she was watched. She glanced
over her shoulder. The creature—it—or she
— made no effort to move, but those fiery eyes
went deliberately from Thora to the meat with
which she was working. And desire was so
plain the girl raised a strip on knife point and
flipped it to her charge.

Claws moved faster than she would have
thought possible, seizing upon the morsel. The
bite was chewed, swallowed and the hand held
out again. Once more Thora supplied a strip.
This one was consumed more slowly, as if the
creature savored as it ate.

There was not another gesture. Apparently
the other was now satisfied. The girl offered a
pannikin of water and those claws took it from
her, the tongue lapping busily until the cup
was held up for more.

Thora dressed herself and settled cross-legged by the fire. There must be some way of communicating with the creature. Body movement meant much to Kort—could that be a way? Or did this oddity have speech—some common tongue with man? She was sure it was not of her species, but it must walk erect, its head was large and well shaped, there was intelligence in the way it watched her, made known its wants.

She cleared her throat. It was so seldom that she spoke these days. Usually she said only the rituals and prayers at the proper times, that she might not forget what was so needful. For it was the sound of such words as well as their meaning which counted in the Rising Up Ceremonies. Now she felt oddly self-conscious as she said, pointing to her own breast:

"Thora."

Though the creature had cried out in its pain and sickness, it had not uttered a sound since it had regained consciousness and the girl was unsure whether it ever did so by nature. Those dark lips now made no movements to shape words—

For a long moment, red eyes studied the girl. Then one of the claw hands arose. Instead of pointing to itself—the direction of that gesture was to the Chosen mark Thora wore in sight, for her jerkin was still unlaced and the crescent mole easy to see against her light body skin. She saw the jaws of the other gap, the tongue, which was over long and must lie normally coiled behind the teeth, flickered out. That strip of dark flesh was arrow-tipped and it fluttered up and down as she had seen the tongues of serpents move.

Still there was nothing reptilian about this stranger. Back and forth moved that tongue as if its owner was struggling with great effort. Then came a hissing with such a guttural distortion the girl barely caught what might be a word—or a name—a name of power!

"Hhhkkattta—"

Thora's hand flew to her birth marking. That this one knew that Name! Truly all things which moved, and breath and life, were children of the Mother. But to hear that name so—She answered with another Name—one of the inner circle—the way of day and not of night:

"Ardana."

Again the tongue writhed as if it must catch hold upon a word—to drag it forth from a laboring throat which was plainly never meant to shape human speech:

"Sissiterrr—" Slurred and mangled though that was, it made sense.

Thora pointed to the sky which was now indeed deepening into twilight where they could see it through the tree branches.

"Moon—" It was waning, but still it had the power in it.

The creature raised its head a fraction and nodded. Though that seemed to have exhausted it, for it fell back, its hands lying limply across its body, touching its fur covered, shrunken breasts. Then once more the tongue worked and one hand arose to touch claw to breast.

"Malllkin—"

Was that its own name, or the designation of its kind? Thora had no idea. But she nodded vigorously, pointing once more to herself and repeating her name. Then to the other and saying:

"Malkin."

Moved by some impulse she could not explain, she stood up and loosened her belt, turning the top of her breeches down about her hips to display the moon gem.

The red eyes, sighting that, blazed—it seemed to Thora—with actual fire. Then both claw hands came up and moved slowly, but with the ease of long knowledge through certain gestures—two of which brought a gasp from Thora. Those were private things, signed only by the High Priestess (she who was possessed by the Lady when there was great need). The others were strange, but between this stranger who was not born of man and woman, and herself—yes, there was a common heritage, an unbreakable bond.

Their camp in the copse could only be a temporary one. Thora had no idea when another party of traders might come to the rest stop of the building. She traveled a short distance

along the road, sighting there the dried dung
of ponies, as well as the scuffed marks of
boots. There had not been rain for some time;
those had been set there when the ground was
muddy. She sent Kort to scout for a distance
but he reported nothing of any recent passage.

While Malkin lay gathering strength, Thora
set about drying the meat in strips. But also
the girl slipped down to make a more detailed
search of the building. There was no covering
on the bunks—save a malodorous tangle in the
one where she had found Malkin. When she
gingerly twitched that out on the floor she
found it to be a very finely woven weather
cloak—three thicknesses quilted together.

This she brought to the stream side, working over it with wads of scrub grass, sinking it
at last into the stream to be further scoured
clean by running water. It was while she was
about this task that she discovered its inner
lining was worked with thick, colored thread,
the patterns making her start in surprise, peer
the closer, even trace some with fingertip.

Here were her own moon signs, but with
those a spiralled circle which she puckered
forehead over—knowing it must be a sign of
power but not one used by those who had
taught her. There were other symbols, too, the
crossed spears with a surmounting horn
which belonged to the Hunter—the Winter
King.

The cloak had plainly never been made for

Malkin. Even when Thora drew it about her own shoulders the hem swept the ground. It was a garment of ceremony, but whoever had worn it must have been tall and broad of shoulder. As she shook it out Malkin's eyes blazed once more in that fiery brilliance which Thora was sure expressed emotion the other could not or would not communicate otherwise.

Though she had opened the two other doors leading out of the great room in the traders' rest she had found nothing but bare chambers. Perhaps these served as storage chambers. Sometimes the traders were rumored to hold back part of their stock in well guarded places, taking with them only small loads for trade.

How had Malkin come to be here? Traders did not deal in living things, guarding jealously even their beasts of burden which were well trained to trailing. Sometimes they had a hound such as Kort, but those were never sold or bargained for—they were too highly esteemed. People (Thora classed Malkin as that) were not items of trade. So why had this furred, silent creature been abandoned here?

On the third day Malkin moved about restlessly, pulling at the binding on her ankle. Though Thora tried to restrain her, the girl at last gave up the struggle, watched the wrappings she had put on so carefully stripped away. Then Malkin set about working over her own hurt, taking her toeless foot between her hands, massaging and bending it.

Thora could sense the pain that manipulation caused the other. Still Malkin continued with determination. And Thora did not try to interfere. Fresh meat provided by Kort, who brought in small kills, seemed to revive the furred one amazingly. Thora's own revulsion at the manner of Malkin's feeding died away. It was really no different than Kort's; only because the furred one was humanoid in appearance did it bother her.

They were five days in the copse camp. On the night of the fifth the waning moon was narrowed to a thin slit in the sky. Now it would disappear, and with it the strength which Thora believed she could call upon. At the rise of that crescent she threw aside her clothing and walked into the open. The rituals she knew she had mainly watched, only a few of them had she ever taken part in at the Craigs. But, since her wandering westward, she had not neglected any that she knew or could improvise upon. This was not the fullness of the ripe moon, but it was the Last Light before the rebirth of the Maid.

Beneath her feet the new growing grass was soft as she walked first that Path, seeing in her mind Tall Stones which were not here, but which must each be saluted in turn. She faced the Nameless Lords, the Four Watchers. Though those she dared not invoke. However she hummed the Drawing Song, the invocation to HER ABOVE ALL. The old ache, the lack stirred painfully within her. If only she had been Blessed before she had been set adrift . . .

Then—

It was neither a whistle nor a hiss—only a sound as thin as the lightest of breezes. The faint notes of it rose and fell with a cadence which Thora had never heard. Her body answered before her mind was aware of what she did. She dipped and swayed, twirled, turned, foot forward, foot back, caught in the net of that sound as securely as a salmon might be caught in a net set in the spawning river. The sound was so low that at times it echoed more in her head than in her ears—

She moved faster and faster until, turning her head up to the sky, it seemed that the star points shining there were spinning too, following also the bidding of that singing. For singing it was even if it came from no human throat.

Round she went, following the sunpath, pausing at each Watcher's point, north, east, south, west. About her waist the chain slipped and there was a radiance growing. The moon jewel flashed as she moved. Thora did not even feel the grass beneath her feet. Instead she was free, as if flesh and bone, all which made up Thora, had grown as light as some wind-carried seedling reft away from the earth to be born up to the very sky throne of the Mother.

2

Even as it had slowly caught her by its rhythm, so did the song to which she was captive begin to die. Moisture dropped from her chin, to spatter on her breast as Thora stood quiet, her body bathed in sweat in spite of the now-chill night wind. Both arms and legs felt leaden, as if she had used them for some task which had pushed her to the very edge of endurance. She raised one arm slowly to draw the back of her hand across her face, pushing away the hair plastered to forehead and cheeks.

Thora felt as one fresh awakened out of a deep sleep—a sleep in which now-forgotten dreams had moved. She saw Malkin dully. The furred one was seated on the cloak—it spread wide with that many-patterned inner surface up. Between her claws the other held a length of reed such as could be culled from any stream side. As Thora stared Malkin dropped that from her wide mouth where her tongue no longer caressed it. So quiet was it now—in spite of the wind—that Thora heard a crunch as the pointed teeth crushed the reed. Malkin spit the bits into a narrow palm which closed about them tightly.

The red eyes flamed so Thora would not have believed those of any living creature might do. She was certain that actual radiance fanned out from each. Then the lids half closed, and Malkin's shoulders hunched, as if the wind were becoming too strong for her bone-thin body.

Thora's very bones ached. She had felt this way before when she had tramped all day on some hard road trail. Pain gathered about her hip joints as she took one stiff step and then another towards Malkin, her arms swinging, dead weights, by her sides. Though never had she been so exhausted as this, still she felt no touch of evil such as she had been warned against.

Thus step by weary step she came to the furred one, standing before Malkin where she sat cross-legged on the cloak with the authority of an Old One. Malkin's own hand came out, gripped the swinging moon jewel. The gem within it was aglow, alive, with light. Malkin did not try to take it from the girl, only cupped it in her own hands. Though, Thora realized at that moment, the virtue had so been drawn out of her that she could not have defended her precious thing even if Malkin had reft it from her.

Instead she stood quietly while the furred one held the pendant so. Then Thora knew —into that gem of the Mother's bestowing she had danced all the power which her own spirit and energy could draw. Now from it Malkin, in turn, was draining that into her own furred self—another form of feeding—or rebuilding.

Nor could Thora deny the other that nourishment. She had never known of such a ceremony as this. But she was only partially an initiate. What was done among the Tall Stones at certain times only those with the full knowledge could say. Malkin had used her to produce this strength, as if by right.

The furred one released the pendant which no longer glowed. Thora wilted to her knees. Putting out a hand to steady herself, her palm pressed upon the cloak. She uttered a sharp cry. It had not been cloth she had touched then—rather a source of warmth—as if she had rested her hand against some living entity.

On her knees, her head was nearly at a level with Malkin's. Now the other put forth both thin hands, the claw tips of her fingers just touching, sliding across the girl's forehead, down her cheeks, to flutter across her lips. It was a gesture of caress, a kind of greeting—a thanks—

Malkin moved a little aside, drew Thora forward so that she, too, sat on the cloak. The warmth of it arose above her. Nor did she really know when she crumpled down, to lie in a curl, while the furred one sat beside her, slowly, gently, brushing the hair back from the girl's forehead, the long tongue flickering in and out between her jaws, her red eyes half-lidded. So Thora slept.

She awoke suddenly in the light of predawn. The cloak was now wrapped around her and for a moment or two she was dazed, for there was a maze of fast fleeting dreams behind her—strange dreams of singing, and another who had leaped high over a fire, bright steel in hand, spinning, smiting at the air, as if he battled fiercely the unseen. Now as the girl lay blinking into the lighting sky she sought to hold to that picture. Only it shredded from her, as dreams so often did.

Kort stood over her, his nose against her cheek. Deep in his throat sounded the rumble of a growl. Instantly Thora pushed aside the dream as well as the cloak. Caution awakened. She threw herself upon the pile of clothing she had discarded the night before, at the same time using eyes, ears, nose, to test the world around. Malkin stood with her back to the girl, facing in the direction of the building—though there was a screen of tree and brush to hide it. In her hands she held the second of Thora's throwing spears, not fitted to its hurling stick, but rather as an in-fighting weapon. As the girl came up beside her she glanced up and radiated, in a way Thora could not understand only acknowledge, not only a strong sense of danger, but also hate tinged with fear.

Thora caught sound, the thud of pony hooves, a mutter of distant voices. People were on the road, undoubtedly heading for the traders' rest. She moved with speed. Much of the meat, only half-cured, must be left. What she could take she bound up in the hide of her kill. Her shoulder pack was already together, for never did she neglect that precaution along the trail.

She looked doubtfully at Malkin. The furred one had rolled the cloak, was tying the ends, before slipping the circlet of cloth over one shoulder. But was her ankle strong enough for the going? And if they had to take to real flight—

Kort surprised her then. He moved in beside Malkin, his head near on the level with that of the furred one. She threw an arm across his back and he matched his steps to hers, supporting her weight as she limped along.

Thora followed, after shouldering both of her packs. There was no time to conceal the camp site. But she could depend upon Kort's wisdom to guide them into the best hiding place which could be found. He was ahead making a slow way to favor Malkin, farther

into the small wood. Under the trees the
ground began to rise. Thora played rear
guard, using all she knew to disguise their
passing. But if these strangers had companionship of such as Kort, what she did would
count as nothing.

There came a loud bray. So those travelers
must have the small donkeys who could carry
such heavy burdens—as well as ponies—in
their train. Traders then, for raiders did not
use such animals. The day grew lighter and the
girl watched Malkin anxiously, wondering
how, even with Kort's support, the furred one
could keep going. Her limp was pronounced,
and now she used Thora's second spearbutt
down as a staff.

They had advanced for a time before Thora
discovered that under the drifted leaves of last
season there was so firm a footage that they
must be following a road such as the Ones Before had once laid down. The taller trees grew
in lines, leaving mainly brush and saplings between.

Kort, during his explorations, must have
chanced on this, though why he selected this
direction now Thora could not guess—save
she depended on him. The land immediately
ahead was banked on either side by a rise yet
higher. Here the drift of soil and leaves had
not been so deep that she could see at times
the dark of the roadway.

Thus they came out into a hollow where

there were the remnants of another building. Only time had not dealt so well with this one. For there was left only a crumple of walls, some pits in the earth. Thora would have skirted this, seeing more of a trap than a shelter. However Kort headed for one of the cellar pits.

He looked back from its edge to the girl, his message plain in a slow swing of his head as he looked down into the dark opening and then back again to her. Kort was urging descent into the earth.

Shucking off her pack and the unwieldy bundle of the meat and hide, Thora came level with the hound and the furred one to look down in turn. The darkness was daunting and she hesitated. Kort's lip lifted—he was growing impatient. Only because of her trust in him did she yield.

Brush and saplings hung over the edge, a veil shadowing much which was beneath. However a tree, storm struck seasons ago, cleared a space. Thora went to her knees by that, sweeping aside a clump of tall-stemmed weeds, now able to see that here was a flight of stairs—covered with moss and a greenish slimelike growth.

She signalled to Kort and Malkin to remain, and, spear ready, she slipped over, descending into a twilight gloom. It was not a long stair. Perhaps ten steps brought her onto a firm pavement. Once her eyes adjusted to the

gloom she saw a mass of debris reaching
nearly to where she stood. Beyond that was a
black hole which surely had been uncovered
by the fall of that—not a hole but rather a
door, for the sides of the opening were regu-
larly cut.

Thora had no desire to push on blindly into
the dark, even with Kort to reassure her. However there were lengths of wood, old but still
firm enough to be bound into a torch, and in
her belt pouch was a striker box to spark that
flame. She stood at the bottom of the stair and
beckoned to the other two.

Malkin loosed hold on the dog, waited, balancing with one hand on the wall and the other
on the spear, while Kort rolled both packs
down to Thora. At the foot of the steps he
waited for the girl to knot the hide and meat
burden to his back, then, with a flirt of his tail,
went confidently on through that waiting
doorway.

Thora was gathering wood for her proposed
torch when a clawed hand caught at her wrist
and she looked to see Malkin shaking her head
firmly. Instead the furred one opened her eyes
wide, blinked several times as if to direct the
girl's attention to them, plainly suggesting
that Malkin, for one, needed no such light.

Thora hesitated. The fewer signs of their
passage which they left behind them the better. But those slippery steps and the slow way
Malkin had descended them was a warning.

Thora sent her one spear thudding into its carrier and held out her arms. She gathered up the other, the warm fur soft against her arms, as she carried her new companion as she might a child.

Once across the pile of debris the furred one twisted and signed to be put down, as one confident of being able now to manage. Kort, waiting just inside that doorway, once more moved to her side and they started ahead. There was something odd. It took a space of several steps for Thora to realize that the cloak which Malkin wore tied around her was giving off a ghostly aura of light.

What had been woven into that? To the girl the fabric had seemed very like any that she knew—save perhaps smoother and finer of weave. This light was thin, only showing a portion of Malkin's and Kort's outlines—but it was a beacon she herself could follow.

Once Malkin looked back. Her eyes were so brightly ablaze—more brilliant than Thora had ever seen them—that the girl was amazed. It would seem that the furred one *DID* have her own method of seeing in the dark.

Away from the entrance the floor was very smooth and unencumbered with any loose stone. Thora stooped once and ran her finger tips along it. The pavement was surely not stone and she wished she had more light to see it better.

She had no idea how long they traveled that

underground way before the haze which marked Malkin and Kort halted. Then she heard that hissing speech—a word repeated several times as she caught up:

"Doooor—"

The other two stepped aside to let Thora approach the barrier. She put out her hands to run those over what seemed at first to be a wholly smooth surface. Then at waist level, she came upon a projection in the form of a wheel. There were spaces along the edge of that into which her fingers seemed to slip of their own accord. Tightening hold she tried to turn it—first one way and then the other. She had never seen such a locking device in use before but those of the Before Time had many lost secrets.

This resisted her efforts and she began to believe that there was no way of loosening the lock. They would have to retrace their path. Then, out of the shadows, behind her there arose the same kind of low crooning as had set her dancing beneath the waning moon. This time it did not woo her into any movement of body or feet, but rather it appeared to strengthen her in her battle with the wheel.

Thora threw her full strength in that direction which came natural, the sun's path. It seemed locked forever. Then—so suddenly that she was near spun off her feet—the resistance of ages broke, the wheel turned—only a fraction to be sure. But, so encouraged, Thora bent her whole strength to its subjection. There was a grating, harsh enough to drown out the song.

It had come near completely around now. Also she could urge it no farther. Still holding on, she pulled, dragging it toward her. Again she met resistance. But Thora fought on, varying a steady pull with sudden short vigorous jerks. It began to yield gradually. There puffed out at them air which was less chill, less tainted with the scent of mold.

Shaking from her efforts, Thora moved aside to allow Kort to brush past her. She felt Malkin's claws gain a hold on her belt. Together the furred one and Thora forced their way through that narrow opening into a burst of light, as if a torch had been put to the flame by their coming.

Before them now stretched a hall without any breaks in the smooth walls. Those walls were fashioned of a smooth blue-green substance like metal, and all about was fresh air and light. Though there was no sign from whence those came. Above all lay a brooding silence through which Thora fancied she could hear their own breathing. Kort's spine hair was up a fraction, his dark lips wrinkling back, and the girl's unease matched that of the hound.

Malkin twitched away the vine wrap tie of the cloak she carried. With a quick flip of the wrist she sent the fabric swinging out, to lie open on the floor, going down on her knees at the edge of its expanse. From the searching look she gave it she might be now consulting a map.

Briskly she patted out a fold so that all the symbols were fully revealed. This being so, she extended one hand very close above the surface, moving her flattened palm back and forth, now pausing for a moment above one symbol or another. Though Thora could not understand the purpose of this she shifted the burden of her pack and stood quietly waiting. A clicking brought her head up.

Kort's nails sounded on the substance of the way as he continued on, his head up, plainly testing for scent. Perhaps he so picked up emanation far beyond Thora's detecting, for from his throat, came a low growl—a warning caution—but not yet an urge to prepare for battle.

Whatever Malkin sought in the cloak she could not find. At last she sat back on her heels, looking up to the girl and shaking her head in a very human gesture of bafflement. Then she swiftly rerolled the cloth as Kort went on ahead as if he stalked some quarry.

Malkin caught at Thora's belt once again to steady herself, leaving the hound free to range. He went slowly at first. Then, seeming to make up his mind that no immediate danger lay near, he broke into a trail lope which carried him well ahead into a haze of shadows filling the far end of the way.

That strange veiling of the distance appeared to keep always the same distance from them, as if it moved even as they did. But Kort had disappeared from sight. Thora wanted to give a summoning whistle to bring him back, but a strong instinct against breaking the quiet here prevailed.

They went, but slowly for Malkin's sake, halting now and again—though the furred one uttered no complaint. Twice so they stopped, Thora squatting down while Malkin subsided beside her, rubbing and kneading her ankle.

Then Kort gave tongue—a sharp series of barks startling them. Thora, so well aware of the range of sounds the huge hound could voice, recognized these as expressing excitement at some find—not a warning of danger. Kort did not return, but continued to bark, urging them to join him.

They came to a second door. This had not been sealed, though it had the same wheel-controlled lock. Rather it stood ajar. Kort appeared there, voicing a series of imperative yaps.

At first Thora could not believe that such an open chamber as they now entered could have been fashioned by man—even those of the Before Time who had been masters of such arts as only the Mother-Touched could dream existed. This spread out near as large to her sight as a good quarter at least of the Craig meadows and cultivated fields. There was no open sky overhead as she half expected. That same haze which had blanketed out the far reaches of the hall hung far above—they were still underground.

The floor under them had the same sleek surface of the walls and pavement of the hall. Pillars so thick in girth that perhaps three men clasping hands could not have encircled them formed aisles cutting the endless stretch before them. Between those were lines of things covered with taut pulled material which veiled the true shape of what it concealed.

Kort, after he ushered them in, turned to the left, still urging them to follow, trotting along in the open space between the wall and the beginning of those lines of pillars. Finally he guided them into a section where there were no longer any large shrouded objects—rather piles of boxes and containers set up in orderly fashion, leaving a cleared runway between.

There he halted looking back. Thora dropped her backpack, freeing herself from Malkin's hold on her belt, reaching for her throwing spear. Then she realized that what hunkered there no longer lived.

The body was propped against some boxes which had been pulled out of line and jammed together to form a barricade. Clothing still gave a semblance of life, until one saw that an outflung hand was merely dried skin over bone. But the clothing itself had not been touched by time, having indeed some of the same metallic sheen as the floor and walls. Once, she suspected, it had fitted its wearer near as tightly as his own skin. The head was encased in a round ball of the same material and that had fallen forward so that if that covering had any opening they could not see the face beneath.

There had been little in the past year of her wandering which had left Thora squeamish. She had seen many kills and she had killed in order to live. But there was something alien about this dead one, marking it not of her own world or life. Was this the remains of one of those from the Before Time?

Fallen from the shrunken hand lay a length of metal which she judged to be some type of weapon. He had died alone perhaps—and no one had come to give him burial honors. Had he been the last of his kin? There was no disarray among the boxes about as there might have been if raiders had pillaged here. Thora glanced around—no more bodies—no evidence that this one, in his dying, had taken any enemy with him.

She drew on the air the symbol of honor and peace and the words of leave-taking came to her without conscious calling:

"The One is the beauty of the earth, the green of growing things. SHE is the white moon whose light is full among the stars, soft upon the earth. From HER all things are born, to HER all things, in their season, return. Where there is beauty and strength, there is beauty and rest. Every act of our will, every thought of our minds is returned three-fold to us in this life—that we may be free when our short day is done and the PATH opens before us.

"Let those who sleep, rest in beauty, to wake in full strength once again—to stride among the stars, spread wings on fresh winds, know and see, where before they abode in ignorance and blindness, being as but children.

"Long ago did you depart, stranger. May you walk on the PATH with swift, joyful feet, looking back upon this sleep as a dream which no longer concerns the you eternal—"

Though this one may not even have known the Lady, still it was fitting that she say these things. While Kort, as if he shared that strange feeling of loss, threw up his head. From his throat came a long, echoing howl—the spirit cry of his own people.

3

The hound did not approach the dead. Rather Kort circled about the body to set off down the aisle which that unknown had guarded. Raising up her pack Thora prepared to follow, feeling Malkin's claws scrape her jerkin as the furred one, too, again grasped a belt hold. The girl stepped out more briskly when they had left the defender well behind, though she kept on the lookout for any more signs of old struggle here.

What had been the purpose of this place, she wondered? Had this been a huge storage depot for traders? What a wealth of materials must be here. And for how long had they lain so?

Her throat was parched and she was hungry. Malkin, in spite of her brave efforts, was dragging of pace now. They must rest, eat, drink from Thora's water bottle. Kort perhaps agreed with that thought for he stopped in a wider, open space between two lines of boxes to wait for them.

Their supply of water was limited and that worried Thora. Certainly no springs nor streams were to be found here—and could they reach the outer world again? She shared carefully a smaller ration of what sloshed in her trail bottle, pouring Kort's portion into a pannikin for him to lap. Malkin drank easily enough. However, it was plain that the furred one found the portion of half-curled meat Thora offered her hard to swallow.

While Thora was still chewing on her own share, the furred one stood up, shucked off the roll of the cloak she bore, to limp to the wall of boxes beside them. Malkin stooped a little, her head thrust forward, as if she were sniffing, even as Kort might, along the edges of some containers. Kort watched her, his head a little on one side, until she paused, her eyes beginning to glow. Then the hound went to her and pressed his own nose against a visible crack about the edge of a cylinder.

There were markings on the side of that which meant nothing to Thora—no real pattern. The furred one reached with both hands, leaning against other boxes to spare her foot, wriggling loose the container which appeared to be heavier than its size would suggest. The urgency of her desire reached the girl and Thora arose to help swing the cylinder to the floor.

At once Malkin began picking with her claw tips along the thin seam at the top. Thora watched uneasily, having little desire to meddle, until Malkin looked to her appealingly. With a shrug Thora drew her knife and, with care for that old and precious blade, pried at the crack.

She worked it carefully, then inserted the point of one of the throwing spears to apply stronger leverage. Malkin watched eagerly, her tongue flicking back and forth, giving voice to a low hissing.

With a whoosh the cap gave way, to spin off and clatter across the floor. Thora saw within a number of stopped tubes of transparent substance, each filled with a red-brown dust.

Malkin's claws flashed, closed about one of those tubes, to have it out of its cushioned nest almost in a single uninterrupted movement. Holding the tube firmly, the furred one used her teeth to worry off that cap which corked it. Her tongue played out into the tube, caught up the top layer of powder, snapped back into her mouth. She stood for a moment as if she were savoring the taste of something to be greatly relished.

Then she raised the tube a second time, her tongue scouring the contents, lapping that dust as Kort would lap water. Thora had half put out a hand to stop her, fearing that this experiment might be harmful. But the speed of Malkin's avid consumption made any such intervention now useless.

One of the tubes, emptied, was tossed aside. Malkin finished the contents of another before her hunger, or greed, was appeased. She settled down, giving every evidence of one who had consumed something her body had long craved, having taken the powder as a man dying of thirst might have gorged himself on water.

Her eyes had lost their bright glow. The lids drooped as if she were so satiated that she was on the verge of sleep, as would be true of some hunting beast who had gorged his fill. Thora ventured to draw out one of the tubes for herself, snap off the cap, sniff at the contents. There was a faint odor but one she could not place.

Malkin roused again, to spread out the cloak and lift out not only the rest of the vials, but also that protecting padding which had been placed around them, stacking them on the folds of cloth, plainly planning to take them with her. She moved more swiftly, favored her foot less. It was as if she had found a sustenance, healing and energy-renewing, in those tubes.

Kort had trotted on a few paces. Now he looked back and whined. With an inward sigh, Thora shouldered her pack, waited for Malkin to take the belt hold. But the furred one moved out on her own after the dog with a much-lessened limp.

There was no night nor day here. That dusky, grayish light (of which Thora never discovered the source) remained constant. Only her tired body let her know that they had, some time later, come to the end of a day's travel. She had dropped behind, was looking for a camping place, when once more Kort's summoning bark rang out loudly enough to make her hurry on.

He had reached the other side of this huge storehouse at last. Before was another wall —with no doorway. Thora saw Kort, nose to the floor as if he now trailed with a clear scent, again turn left, padding along the open stretch by the wall. There was no dust in which any footprint might be marked, yet the hound appeared certain of his way.

Thora and Malkin hurried after. The furred one's eyes began to glow once more. There was an eagerness and purpose which matched Kort's in her progress. Thora was tired and longed to call a halt. However Kort had ranged far ahead, only his impatient barks kept them in touch.

Thus he brought them into a true battlefield, where death had walked long since. Once more they saw a barricade of tumbled boxes and containers. Many bodies sprawled here. Yet all lay on the other side of the barrier and here there were no signs of any defenders—Nor did these dead wear the ageless clothing of the sentinel they had found earlier.

Rather their limbs were covered with rags, stained, tattered, a travesty of clothing, such as might serve as body covering for the survivors of some great disaster, people who had been driven back into a feral existence. Uncovered heads were turned up—to make Thora shudder. For, long dead though these were, they wore the marks of madness and terror. The weapons which lay among them were knives bound to branches of decaying wood to serve as crude spears, clubs with rusty spikes protruding from them, even rudely shaped stones bound to hafts, like axes.

They lay without dignity, in no order. Thora had a mind picture of mad creatures coming in a wave of assault—to whom death had been a blessing.

Only among them was a single body, well to the rear of those who had faced so fatally the defenders of that barrier. Unlike the others in that company it was not clad in rags. Rather lying over it, to conceal most of what lay beneath, was a cloak—the edge of that spreading out like the wings of a bird across the floor.

The cloak was bright red—a screaming scarlet which might have come from being dipped in the free flowing blood of those about it. It was also richly glowing—the fabric from which it had been fashioned the finest of weaving.

Thora stood looking upon this battle site. Nothing of compassion moved in her, as it had upon sighting that other they had come upon. There was no stir of kinship here—rather was born a horror which grew even as she looked, something which denied the cleanliness and finality of death.

Malkin threaded a path among the fallen to the side of that cloaked body. With a quick flick of claws she jerked up and back the nearest edge of that covering to display its lining, though not the body.

Here were embroidered patterns such as lined the cloak she herself carried. But these symbols were strange. To gaze at them made Thora uneasy, so that she was glad when Malkin dropped the cloth and they were again hidden from view. If one could sense such, and Thora knew that the initiated could do so, evil hung here now like a noxious vapor which even time had not been able to dissipate.

Deliberately the furred one worked her mouth, her purple lips tight together. Then she spat—straight at the hooded head of the dead. She hissed, striving very hard to twist her tongue about a word, bring that forth so Thora could understand.

"Ssssettt—" Her mouth worked as she tried again. "Sssettt—"

Thora flinched. If she had interpreted that aright—!

He-Who-Abode-in-the-Dark, ruled the Left Hand Path—who gave birth to evil, beguiled men to foul ways—

"Set!" the girl repeated in a low whisper. Her hand moved in the ancient sign of warding. In truth she had found Old Evil here if one who had spoken for that power lay before her, dead or not.

Thora wanted to flee that place of battle. Could fear and evil lash out at the living from such a place? There was a belief among all who were followers of HER that an object might gain stronger reality, greater power, if it was to confront any such force, good or evil. Now she shrank back from that cloak, afraid that the gem she wore in concealment, her own small power, might bring into half-life some of this malignity.

She gestured to Kort fiercely to go. Malkin watched with fire pit eyes in which Thora could read no human emotion. Now as the furred one came away from the Dark Dead, her tongue moved. Thora waited for a struggling word but none came.

Kort trotted on, Thora followed, not waiting for Malkin to catch up. Luckily there was escape from this underground prison in sight now—Kort sniffed at a break in the wall. That itself was rent apart, earth and stones had cascaded out into the storage place, leaving a dark hole.

There was a scent here, too, a dank mustiness Thora did not like. Kort growled as Malkin pushed up beside him. She still carried the throwing spear she had used as a staff and this she swung point forward.

"Out!" The fear which had been seeded at Malkin's recognition of the scarlet cloaked dead grew fast in Thora. She had no doubt that both of her companions were wary of something ahead, only it was better to face the unknown that any remnant of the DARK. The girl wanted passionately to be above ground where the *Sign* of the *Lady* rode the night sky and there was nothing of ancient evil.

Kort growled again, but he did not refuse to enter the hole, rather he crawled up the fall of earth and stone and shouldered on into the shadowed space. While Malkin appeared as willing to face what might lie there. Thora loosed the pack from her back so that she might go more easily through the break.

Here were no lighted walls. Again the faint radiance of Malkin's rolled cloak was her only guide. She swept the path before her with her own spear, fearing a misstep. The footing was rough so she went carefully, hearing the scrambling and scuffling of her companions. Then there *was* a wan light—far ahead. They might be making their way not along a passage, but in a narrow cleft with the night sky above.

Kort gave a great rasping howl. Warning enough for Thora to set back to the wall, pack

thrown aside, spear and knife ready. There
came a scrabbling, growls from Kort, a flurry
of what must be a fight. A musky stench envel-
oped the girl as she caught sight of small
points of light near the ground—eyes?

To Kort's growls was added a hissing she
was sure came from Malkin. Then followed a
shrill squealing. Thora braced herself, struck
down at the pair of eyes within reach. Her
spear entered flesh; there was another squeal
of pain. Thora jerked free the spear to strike
again. That which she attacked was gone, but
another leaped upward, scored a burning
slash along her arm. She used the knife, felt
blood, warm and foul smelling, gush over her
hand. Knife—spear—still the attackers came.

Her arm burned but she had not dropped
her weapon. Thora had no time—already another was on her. Still the snarling and hissing
assured her that her companions were fighting on.

Then that hissing arose to an ear-torturing
sibilance which made Thora cry out, for the
sound seemed to bite into her brain. She staggered, feeling as if the bones of her skull were
being forced apart.

Dazed now, she could only huddle back
against the sour earth, clinging still to
her weapons, though her body shook to the
rise and fall of that sound. There were no
more eyes. The squealing grew weaker—or
perhaps it was drowned out by Malkin's

throat wrenching cries.

Was it quiet at last, or had hearing failed her? Thora was only fully aware of the pain in her head. Then there was a touch on her tooth-lacerated arm. She tried to flinch away. That grip tightened, pulling her on.

Her boots trod on softness—bodies? She stumbled, was jerked up and ahead. In a daze of pain she followed. For how long she did not know nor care—all she wanted was relief from the agony in her head.

Cool wind on her face, allaying that agony a little. Then she toppled forward into space, struck against earth, only to slide into complete darkness.

Thora stood at a clearly marked crossroads where three well-worn paths met. Standing at their centerpoint, stark and grim, was a hewn form so long settled there that its feet had become one with the earth itself. Around it grew a long hedging of tall plant stalks, withered and dead, as if the carven countenance above had blasted them out of life.

Fungi clung to the statue itself, loathsome yellow-green patches like the markings of a fell plague. The face, with blind blank eyes, bore across it, from forehead to sharp, out-pointing chin, a crack, distorting even more the malice and hatred suggested by that carving.

This—this was the Dark Side of the Mother—that part of HER which took pleas-

ure in slaying. So was this representation of
HER ever set at ill-famed crossroads. There
followed a stirring among the dead weeds, as
from there emerged grey things with bared
fangs. These were not common rats, but rather
huge monsters of their species. Dappled they
were with scabs and sores, and their eyes were
afire with greed and hunger as they pattered
towards Thora.

She strove to lift spear, knife. But her arms
were weighted; she could not stir.

Still within her was life and to her could
come death—perhaps not of the body, but of
that which was there encased during this lifetime. Thora cried out, a mindless, wordless
scream, as the first of the rats sprang.

Light lanced from the right-hand pathway.
Along that beam of light sped things fashioned
of pure flame, white as the Mother in the full
glory of Her High Nights. These leaped into
the air, some hurtling straight towards the
statue, others at the foul flood of rats.

From where they struck came bursts of pure
light. That did not sear Thora's eyes. Rather it
was warmth, healing, soft—caressing—

The rats the lance light touched—were not!
Where it fastened on the statue there was born
a glow which ate up the patches of foul lichen,
producing a silver shining. The eyes in the
face were no longer blankly dead—they had
become pure and glowing moon gems—
larger and more beautiful than any the girl

had ever seen.

That scar crack drew together, and now lips which were no longer dull stone, curved into a faint smile. The beam of light down which the sparks raced still held. Along it moved another, taller, manlike, wearing a cloak of deep green, which flapped and flared about his body as he moved. Only there was a haze which helmeted his head, hid his features.

There was no crossroads, no statue. She was staring up at a sky where dark clouds massed, and on her face was a pelt of rain which came in slanting waves to fold about her. Dull pain still held in her head and when she turned that a fraction it stabbed more sharply.

Kort's head loomed into her range of sight. He stooped to set his teeth in her jerkin, taking so tight a grip that she felt the score of his fangs on her skin. A claw hand joined, and then another, to catch at her shoulders. Together the hound and Malkin dragged her over rough ground, jolting so painfully she cried out.

Now there was an overhang of stone above her. The rain no longer soaked her body. Thora drew a deep breath and raised a hand feebly, striving to urge Kort to loose her. But he had already done so. Sitting back on his haunches he looked down into her face. Malkin moved to her other side. Thora realized that the sleeve of her jerkin was torn and that her left arm now lay across the furred one's knee, Malkin was spreading on a bloody wound there some of Thora's own healing salves.

So clear had been her vision of that otherwhere, that Thora, when she could brace herself up on one elbow and look out of the shallow cave her companions had found, searched for the statue, the crossroads. However, what lay beyond was wild country with no suggestion that anyone had ever passed this way before.

Malkin, having finished tending Thora's wound, leaned forward. Her eyes did not blaze now, but still they compelled in a way which made Thora meet that gaze squarely. She felt giddy, as if for a breath or two she had been whisked across a gulf at the bottom of which lay nothingness. Then once more she was at the crossroads, though seemingly held at a point in the air above it. She saw a dim form in the place where she herself had once stood——a form which rippled and wavered. Once again the rats emerged from the weeds, crouched to spring.

The flash of light followed and along it sped the sparks. But these were clearer now—smaller than Malkin, yet their brilliance was wrought into the forms of the furred ones.

From this height Thora perceived the source of that beam. A sword planted point down in the earth, its pommel a crystal. It pulsated with light, sending the beam. From behind the weapon moved a human form, distorted somewhat as if she viewed it through eyes which were not really hers.

She saw the high-held head—no haze to conceal it now. Human—a man—young and yet not young—ageless. There was a cap of short dark hair above a wide brow, and in that hair was entwined a crooked circlet of the *Lady's* own silver—as if a briary branch had been wreathed and then hardened into metal. Along it showing the soft sheen of moon gems. His flesh was moon-white also—heavy brows and long lashes so overhung his eyes that those might have been mask-hidden. There were sharp lines about nose and mouth, giving him a resolute and commanding countenance.

Along the beam he went and—

The vision broke for the second time. She was looking at Malkin. The furred one moved her mouth convulsively, her tongue twisted in and out, while her eyes blazed with such fire that Thora almost expected real flames to issue from them.

"Who—?" Thora must have an answer. It was very true that the Mother spoke to her Chosen in visions, though almost always those were deliberately sought after ceremonies and fasting. That she had just been given one, when she was no full priestess, nearly violated everything she had been taught. "Who—" she began again, "is he who walks in the sword light?"

Malkin's hands pressed tightly against her

small, down-covered breasts. Her tongue curled, straightened again as might a lashed whip. Still her eyes blazed.

"Maaakilll—" The effort had been great but she had said the word at last.

"Makil?" Thora tried to repeat it carefully.

Malkin nodded violently. Her hands fluttered and she pressed the heels of her palms against her eyes. To Thora's astonishment she saw slow drops of moisture slide from under them down the furred cheeks. Malkin was crying!

The girl sat up in spite of the pain in her head, the twinge in her arm. She reached out to take those claws into her own fingers, hold them close.

"Who—?" She began and then changed her question. "What is Makil?"

Malkin pulled one of her hands from Thora's grasp and patted the cloak which was never far from her.

"Maaakillll!"

Thora knew the possible power of that symboled cloak. He who would wear such was near to a full priest, if not equal to her own Three-In-One. But the Hunter, in spite of his being the Winter King, never claimed such power. She had never heard of any man who followed the deep rituals. And that vision —surely that had been in another world, one in which the Mother reached, yes, but perhaps only in *HER* darker aspect. Still the sword holder had brought light into darkness there. No *man* could do that—!

The girl felt a flash of anger. Still she dared not deny the vision. To do that was to deny the very power which was the core of her life. She longed for clearer communication with Malkin. Though this Makil meant so much to the furred one he was plainly not of her own species. What was the tie between the two?

Malkin fought for speech again. She had freed her other hand and now she pointed to her own breast.

"Maaakill—Malllkinnn—" she held up two of her very slender fingers pressed tightly one to the other, "Ssssistterrr — shadowww — fam — familiarrr!"

Thora gasped. Old lore—legends—stirred deep in her mind. Only—she stared into Malkin's eyes. Familiars—those were of the Dark Path!

Perhaps the other was able to grasp the girl's thought, for Malkin shook her head violently. Her fingers moved now in the age-old sign of warding off evil and her mouth twisted as it had before she spat upon the wearer of the red cloak.

Before Thora knew what she would do the furred one flung herself at the girl, jerked at the belt of her breeches, drawing those down to expose the moon gem. Malkin's claw fingers hooked about that—then deliberately she brought it so into her palm and closed her hand upon it, her eyes on Thora's.

As carefully as she had caught it up, she let it go again and then turned up, into Thora's full sight, her own hand so that the girl could see there was no mark or weal upon it.

"Seee—noooo—hurrrttt—" she said with a kind of defiance and a touch of anger.

4

Thora's tongue swept over her lower lip. No legend—the truth! For let any one of the Dark lay hand so upon a gem which was worn by one of the Lady's own Chosen and there would follow blighting, and a blasting fire. Whatever Malkin might be she did not give homage to Set or any follower of *His*.

"Not the Dark," Thora agreed. "Then where is Makil?"

Malkin's shoulders hunched, her indignation was gone. Once more moisture gathered in her eyes. It was plain that the furred one had lost him who had such a close bond with her.

"Where did you lose him?" Thora asked carefully. She had never tried to discover before from whence Malkin had come, or why she had been left, a wounded prisoner, in the trading station.

"Seeeleeep — darrrk — waakke — Maaakil — gonnne — Hunt—" She caught the cloak to her, hugging its folds tightly.

"Sssseett ones coommeee— Taaakke — Hold — Maaakill Coommme — gettt — theyyy catchh — tryyy sooo—" She struggled to form the words, while flecks of foam gathered in the corners of her wide mouth, spun by her effort.

Thora tried a guess. "Some of the Dark Path took you—would use you as bait to catch Makil?"

Malkin gave a cry of excitement and triumph, nodding her head so vigorously that the brush of her hair floated even more widely about her head. She started to gesture now, as if the struggle to talk was too much for the explanation she needed to make. With motions she suggested tying something about her ankle, then pointed to a tree outside their present cave. Her claws flickered as they moved to suggest others in hiding about that.

"Noooo coomeee. Ssseettt waiiite—" Now she made her fingers walk across the ground. Those of one hand representing newcomers, while others fled. With the second group she made again the gesture of loosening her ankle—then she wilted dramatically to the ground, pantomiming one wounded and ill.

Again Thora guessed. "Traders came along,

found you. But why did the traders then leave you alone afterwards?"

Malkin flipped up the edge of the cloak to display its embroidered symbols. She indicated one of the designs—that for the Hunter. Yes, a trader would know but little of the Mysteries, and he would be ready to abandon one who might be connected with a Power he did not understand.

"Fammmiliarr—knoowww sooo—"

Thora could readily understand that. If the men who found Malkin knew certain old tales, their reaction would be close to hers only moments earlier. They would have feared the furred one as they would any they deemed to be of the Dark. They would not kill her, for they would have reason to believe that they would then bring after them any spirit which was human-tied. So they simply left her to the spirits to live or die as those decreed. Yes, that all fitted well together. Though Thora still could not understand this use of familiars, for it was not a part of any ritual of which she had ever heard.

Still this land was very wide. Even traders who traveled far did not know what might lie on the other side of the mountains which were yet some tens of days travel to the west. There might well be places where the LADY had taught her Chosen different ways of life and power—different, but not evil because of that difference. Malkin had clearly proven herself to be of the Light by holding the moon gem.

Which left the rest of the puzzle—what had happened to this Makil? If he were the man she had seen in the vision (and somehow she did not doubt that he was), he was also plainly one who held and used Power. Perhaps he could even stand before the Three-In-One as an equal, strange though that seemed. He was a Chosen, of that she was sure. And if those of the Dark were attempting to entrap him (as they seemed to have used Malkin to do) then that meant there was here some active struggle between the Dark and the Light—no symbolic one such as the ancient ritual told of—rather one with force and purpose. It was said that the Lady wove the lives of her people as if they were threads in cloth, twisting one strand with the other to form a design which only Her eyes might see. Thora shivered.

Surely—surely *she* herself could not be a strand pulled loose from one portion of a pattern to be set elsewhere! She had thought that the raid which had set her wandering had been one of the chances of life. There were always a certain number of homesteads threatened or plundered when winters had been lean. Of late the sea wolves had ventured farther and farther westward: that the Craig dwellers had learned from the traders.

They had raided so often along the shores that men no longer built there, but headed inland for peace. Such groups of refugees had

passed at time through Craig lands—going farther west to claim unused valleys and build
lost fortunes anew.

Without their shore prey the raiders had
taken to rivers—for they were always a water
people. Also they could be sure that any good
sized river would sooner or later have a settle-
ment on its banks. So they had come by stealth
and the Craigs had fallen. For raiders were
warriors and those of the land, while they
were skilled hunters, were not slayers of men.

It had seemed ill-fortune and not by direct
cause that she had so been set adrift. Now
Thora was led to wonder. Her meeting with
Malkin—the discovery of that underground
storage place, the fact that among the old
dead there had lain one who served Set's
Power—was all this part of a new weaving?

The vision—that she must hold in mind as
the priestesses did any true dream, think upon
it carefully. What she had seen was not con-
cise fact, but rather a suggestion of powers at
war and a clear message that she was part of
the struggle. Though it would seem that Malkin's Makil was strong enough to stand
against Dark Forces.

"You seek Makil?" she asked.

Malkin sketched helplessness. Then once
more she fell to stroking the cloak—all which
she had left of the one she longed to be with.
Thora sighed. She looked out into the rain.
Kort had brought in her pack. He must have

gone back into the darkness of the slit and dared face again the danger there to drag it along.

She was tired, hungry, but they were in the open once more and she felt free. Thora dragged the pack to her and began hunting food and water, setting a pannikin out where the steady fall of rain filled it. They drank their fill. The furred one then poured what was over into the trail bottle. She refused the meat the girl offered, drawing instead on one of the vials she had brought out of the storage place, licking at its contents.

Thora would have liked a fire but decided against the comfort of that in unknown territory. So at last they curled up together as far back in the cave as they could squeeze, Kort being gone, Thora guessed to his own hunting. Malkin lay with her head on a double fold of the cloak, the rest pulled about her. Thora watched her settle so with sleep-weighted eyes, wondering if she herself was about to be haunted by some dream vision. She had had enough of those—hopefully for this—or perhaps many other days.

She awoke with the feeling that something waited—some action was demanded of her. Though, if she had dreamed again, no memory remained to guide her. The rain had stopped, yet still there was a massing of clouds that promised more. Again she wished for a fire, yet knew that was folly.

Kort, his coat plastered with mud and water, trotted out of the brush, a rabbit dangling from his jaws. He brought that to Malkin and so they ate. Then Thora climbed a small hillock to see what might lie beyond.

No sign here of any road, still they were on the edge of open country and to travel across that would make them highly visible. She caught sight of willow and other growth bordering what might be a broad river and there were large animals, a herd of them splashing along the edge of the stream.

Now she looked to Kort and made the hand signal which would bring an answer if man were near. The hound continued to lick at one foot to clear mud from between his claws. But he barked once, so assuring her that the land over which he had ranged was clear of her own kind. Still she hesitated—since she had fled the Craigs she had been ever wary of open country.

Returning to the shallow cave she undid her bundles. The poorly dried meat had a bad odor. Though she hated to waste food she dumped that out of the hide which she had scraped and rescraped several times over. Her boots were wearing thin and if they found a safe place to camp awhile she must see to the repairing of them with several thicknesses of hide for new soles.

Repacking her gear Thora settled the familiar burden on her shoulders. Malkin had in turn replaced the vials within the cloak and rolled that into a tight pack. Though the furred one still limped, it was apparent that her injury was healing well. She no longer needed Kort for support, but she retained the spear-staff.

Thora looked back once into the dark throat of the cut from which they had won out of the dark. There was no sign there of any door or opening made by man. Her memory of the fight in the dark was such that she wanted no further exploration there. But she did find, huddled against a rock by the entrance, a creature which brought a lurch of fear to her heart. This was a huge rat such as had crawled from around the feet of the statue in her vision.

It had died snarling, its throat a red ruin. She could believe Kort had tossed it so. Meat eater he was, but such a kill as this was too unclean to tempt him. Nor did she see that it had been disturbed by any of the scavengers which were quick to gather to any kill.

The rain did strike again as they entered the lowlands, but not as a heavy storm, rather a soft drizzle, such as the farmers of the Craigs would have welcomed. This land was greening fast and there were bird songs. Thora held her face up to the sky, relishing the touch of the moisture on her skin. Though Malkin's fur was soon plastered to her body even to that wild mass which crowned her head, she too did not seem to find this a state to cause distress.

Before they reached the river the herd of wild cattle which had drunk there had scattered to graze. They were smaller than those with whom Thora was familiar. And she saw, sharing their pasturage, several ponies of the same breed the traders favored, dun gray of coat. Their manes were ragged and matted, as were their tails, and it was apparent they were not broken to the service of man.

Kort kept well apart from the mixed herd, downwind. He had good reason to be wary of the cattle since they could be formidable opponents, especially with young calves among them. Also there was a bull—and, sighting the toss of that murderously horned head, Thora was very glad they were well away—even though this herd promised fresh meat for a hunter.

The river was pocked by the falling rain, its waters swirling with a lacing of foam about large rocks which broke its surface here and there. Reeds stood tall and other water plants were near submerged to their tops, proving that the flood was above normal. Pieces of tree branch rode the swift central current and among those bobbed a flash of color which caught Thora's eyes.

Against the brownish water, in which mud and soil had thickened the flood, that was so bright it could not be missed. Something tumbled along there. Because it might be of importance to learn more of this land Thora hastily stripped and, with a wave of the hand to Kort, waded in.

The object was still upstream. She thought she might snare it with her spear when it came within reach, though she would not venture into the main current. As swiftly as she might stab at a salmon, she struck for that which she could now see was a roll of stained and muddied cloth.

Thora was nearly jerked from her feet where she stood thigh deep in the river. That wavering strip of cloth was anchored to something far heavier, rolling beneath the surface. She held on, whistling for Kort. The hound splashed in and swam out to the bundle, as the girl fought the pull of the water until he could reach it.

Kort's jaws closed on a mouthful of the cloth, and Thora threw her strength into a pull. Together they worked the bundle out of the main current, into the shallows and so, finally, up on the bank. The cloth was red and badly torn. Beneath its concealment was a shape which Thora found herself oddly reluctant to reveal.

When she knelt to see the better, she caught sight of thongs lashed around and about—an end of one dangled, badly frayed, as if the leather cord had been broken. Perhaps the bundle had been weighted down and the water torn it free.

Kort sniffed and drew back. His head went up and he gave a death howl. Man—no. This was far too small to be the remains of one of her own kind. Thora forced herself to use her knife and saw free those lashings.

Though it required vast determination, the girl tugged at the sodden cloth, peeling it back. Promptly she flung herself away, bile sour in her mouth, as she stumbled farther off still, to lose all she had put in her stomach that morning. The stench seemed to cling to her, so she scrubbed her body with handsfull of grass. When she had herself under control again and returned it was to see Malkin calmly using her spear to drag the rest of the cloth well away.

There was no mistaking what the river had carried. These pitiful remains were those of one of Malkin's people. Also, it was just as plain that death had not come easily. There were wounds enough to show that the furred one had been barbarously used. While the covering which Malkin was now methodically spreading wide was just such a cloak as they had seen on the dead Dark One.

The fabric was badly stained, in places looked charred as if fire had eaten it. There were two blackened holes high on one side—they might have been at heart level for a man.

Malkin regarded the cloak and the thing which had been bound in it. Then she raised brightly blazing eyes. Her tongue flickered out, began those convulsions which proceeded speech.

"Sssettt—wakesss—Seettt walkkks—"

"Who?" The girl gestured to the dead. Did Malkin know him?

"Aaaalkin—brotherrr one—Kaaaarn—likee Maakil—" She labored mightily. Now Malkin swung around to gaze upriver. Though there was nothing in the range of their sight but the water and the land.

"Why?" Thora could not understand the sense of wrapping this dead one (it had been a male) in a covering plainly of the enemy.

"Giveee tooo Ssssett sssooo — killlll — binnnd—keeeppp sssspirit—bound—" Malkin stabbed the edge of the cloak, fury still afire in her eyes. "Deeeaad—ssservess Ssssettt—soooo—"

"A sacrifice to the dead of Set's people?"

Malkin nodded.

Thora tried to remember old tales. Yes, there had even been cases among her own people when the living had believed themselves in bondage to vengeful dead. And if that fear had not been ritually lifted they would have died, sure they were being drawn into the Dark Realm to serve their enemies. Here was evidence of a foul act—killing by torture—of a creature before it was wrapped in a cloak-of-Power, perhaps belonging to the newly dead, so that its life force could be drawn to the Dark.

"No!" The girl rebelled. There was something—if she only knew more! To be on the edge of knowledge and yet lack it—-! Still she was a Chosen and had she only last night not been granted a vision? She wore the *Lady's* gem which by rights only a full priestess could place next to her skin—and the Mother had shown no resentment. Therefore—

Malkin was watching her closely. Thora drew a deep breath. There were two ways of returning to that which had given one birth. Four elements were man's to be used—not misused—earth and air, fire and water. Out of the earth came the harvest—into the fire and water went that which must be cleansed. But she could not use fire here and water had already been profaned—

Or perhaps water had uncovered this evil by the Lady's will. Again she felt that wave of helplessness—that she was caught up in a weaving over which she had no control.

Therefore—it must be the earth which was to receive this remnant of one of the children of the Mother. Into that this torn and battered flesh must be laid so from what was no longer used might spring new life of a different kind.

Thora dressed hurriedly. Then she selected a place beyond the sweep of the hanging willow branches, well above where any flood might reach. There, with the point of her spear, she marked out lines and set to work, cutting and levering out sod.

Clawed hands came to her aid as Malkin knelt and worked with a will, jerking and pulling free the clods. It was a lengthy task when they had only the spears and their bare hands—but at last it was done. Malkin went into the meadow where she twisted free lengths of grass until she had blanketed the bottom of the hole. Thora returned to the other problem. She would not allow the dead to rest in the cloak of the enemy—to do so was to defeat her purpose. So she turned to the willows, began cutting withy lengths which she wove together, sacrificing strips of her hide to tie them into a mat. Then, swallowing her revulsion, and using more willow branches, she moved the body onto the flat bier. Malkin came again to help.

When it lay so Malkin produced three stones from the stream edge, they had been fashioned by the action of the water into discs near as perfect as any gem stone of the Lady's. Two of these she fitted over the pits of the eyes. The other she laid upon the rent flesh of the breast.

Thora dragged the mat to the waiting grave and they lowered it in. More branches were laid across the body and then, working together, they shoveled back the earth and fitted the clods of sod as a cover. The place was not perfectly hidden but with the falling rain and the growing grass it soon would be.

As she knelt beside the grave Thora brought out her gem. She moved it from head to foot,

on the breast level from right to left. From
Malkin came a very low hissing as one who
crooned a lullaby.

But Thora spoke aloud:

"Blessed be, Oh, Mother, for this one was
Thy child—
Blessed his eyes that he saw Thy path and
walked therein.
Blessed his mouth that he praised Thee in
the day and the night.
Blessed his heart that it beat with the life
which Thou gavest him.
Blessed his loins which were fashioned to
bring forth life in Thy honor and to Thy service.
Blessed his feet which walked in Thy path-
ways.
Reach forth Thy loving hand to draw him
into Thy own fair
place where he may rejoice in Thy beauty
and wait until it is
Thy wish that his essence embody again.
Blessed be—in Thy name."

As it had when she had danced beneath the
waning moon so did it now seem to Thora that
the singing of her companion fed and strengthened something deep within her. In those moments she was sure that she had broken
through a barrier and her plea had indeed
risen to the proper place.

Why she did not know, save that the gesture seemed a fitting one—but she reached forth the hand in which the moon gem rested and held it once more over the grave. Out came Malkin's right hand to cover hers so they were palm to palm, the jewel between them.

Then the furred one drew back and Thora also arose. Malkin headed to where the stained cloak still draggled down the bank of the river. She caught it up on the point of her spear and dragged it after her, heading downstream.

Not returning it to the water it had befouled, no. Rather she brought it to a tree which stood stark and dead, no hint of spring-renewing life about it. To the lowest branch of that she endeavored to raise the heavy, sodden folds. Seeing what she attempted Thora hastened to help, together they draped the tattered rag across a dead branch from which it hung in filthy tatters.

Thora desired no camp by the river. She once more shouldered her pack and looking inquiringly to Malkin, sure that the furred one would wish to go on also. Kort who had been ranging the meadowland returned, to face upstream.

Upstream, whence the corpse had come? Thora hesitated—even though she had learned long since to trust the hound. But Malkin also took a step or two in that direction, adjusting the roll of her own cloak about her.

To go into what was not just the ordinary

danger from beast—or of wandering traders— but close to something carrying the rot-
tenness of Set—? That was a decision to be
well considered. Thora's hand sought her
jewel, feeling it beneath her clothing where
she had replaced it. If one had the Leaves of
the Shrine to be tossed and their message
read—only—perhaps in the end those would
have told her the same thing. If there *was* any
purpose to her wandering then it lay in that direction.

Thus they went upstream, winding in and
out among the patches of willow, tangles of
bush and tree. There were game trails in
plenty but nowhere any road. Oddly enough
the farther they drew from the grave the
lighter became Thora's heart, the less her uneasiness of spirit.

She longed for the ability to communicate
freely with Malkin. If she could only learn
more of these "familiars" and of those with
whom they paired! In the old stories of her
people it had been said that so dependent were
the familiars upon their human links that they
could not exist for long away from them. Yet
Malkin had survived and seemed stronger
each day. Therefore that part of the legend
must be false. Only—Thora wanted so much to
understand what fate had overwhelmed Malkin's human—the man of her vision. Had he
been slain? Was he prisoner of Set's forces?
The furred one had indicated that she had

been used as bait to entrap him—that the plan failed with the coming of traders. Thora shook her head—if only she knew more!

Mid-afternoon the rain ceased and the sky lightened. They had come a good distance and Thora was hungry. Even a small evoking of the Power could exhaust one and she had touched on it when she had used her jewel to "seal" the dead.

In spite of her limp Malkin had kept a steady pace. Kort must have gone twice the distance scouting. Now Thora saw him waiting for them at the edge of a thicket which stood before a stand of trees of taller growth than any she had seen.

There was something about those trees— Thora recognized them with a stir of rising excitement. Oaks! Though what such were doing in the middle of this open land she could not understand—unless they had been planted so. She quickened stride, passing Malkin. When she reached Kort she caught a glimpse of grey-white—a stone standing tall among the trees. Then she stopped, her head high. She might not be able to test the wind for scent as well as her four-footed companion, but there was another sense—that which recognized the stir of Power—that might carry either a welcome or a warning.

5

There was a scent borne by the air as Thora went forward slowly. In the grass growing about the bases of the stones shone color—blossoms of white, purple, yellow—violets in such quantities as she had never remembered seeing. And their perfume drove from her the last shadow of the horror she had faced this day.

She approached the nearest stone, trying not to tread upon the clustered flowers. From this point she could see farther into this pocket of woodland. More white stones stood by trees—surely not just by chance. The curled heads of ferns pushed upwards. Here and there in small patches of bare ground lay acorns which displayed no signs of a season's weathering, but rather appeared as if they had fallen only today. Thora's fingers curled about some she stooped to gather. Acorns were a priestess's true jewels, she wore such as a harvest necklace when she surrendered her wand to the Horned Hunter for the winter months.

Cupping the nuts to her breast, the girl went on. Yes, the trees and the stones made a pattern—leading one forward into the heart of this miniature forest. There stood more stones, none marked by man's defacing tools, yet set in a circle for a sky-roofed temple which was truly of the Lady. Thora entered that circle as might a child come safely home, dropping on her knees to the earth where the ground was bare save for a cushioning of moss, soft and brilliantly green.

Kort threw himself down beside her and lay panting, resting his head upon his forepaws as would a hound at his own hearthside. Then Malkin came. The furred one moved with ceremony, facing in each of the Four Directions, her head a little to one side as if she listened. Her tongue flickered ceaselessly but she was not forcing any words. Instead she pulled from her shoulder the roll of cloak, shook out its folds with a whirl of arm so that its symboled side lay uppermost. When that was done to her satisfaction, she seated herself upon it, her hands between her knees.

Peace wrapped them in. Thora wanted to stretch out as she might on a sun touched hillside, unburdened in body and mind. Only Malkin then stirred. Her hands moved in gestures, first slowly, and then with speed, as if what she wrought was an invisible fabric. Also she hummed, her hiss-song growing louder, taking up a more demanding beat.

Thora strove to close her eyes that she might not watch that weaving. It demanded—she even thought she could see faint trailings in the air. The furred one played so with some force. The girl felt strangely light of head—she was being caught in a web.

Then—Malkin brought her outstretched foreclaws together, stabbing down into the center of one of the symbols on the cloak—that of the spiral. She sat silent now, brooding, her talons pricking into the material, her eyes near closed. She might be looking inward, not outward.

Thora had no wish to move, nor speak. Although questions gathered in her mind. However, stronger than any desire for answers was a feeling of expectation growing in her. What would come of Malkin's ritual Thora could not guess. Her fingers brought out the moon jewel, which glowed even though this was only the beginning of twilight.

The girl held the gem tight cupped between palm and palm. Forces were awaking, beginning to seek—No, she did not know what would happen. The gem was still cool yet its light strengthened. Power was gathering.

Again Malkin's fingers moved. From the heart of the spiral she traced its line around and out. Once more she sang. The hair on her head arose from the tight sleek the rain had given it. Each strand quivered, twisted. Thora could feel a tingling along her own skin. Fear, yes—that tugged at her but that was only part of it. She was on the edge of something which perhaps only the Three-In-One among her own people knew.

Round and round went those fingertips, outwards—an untying—a loosening. There was a drift of hazy smoke following that touch. When Malkin raised her hands a cone of vapor poured upward from the symbol. Pale against the dark cloak, against Malkin's own fur, it was plain to see.

That cone began to swirl though Malkin no longer guided it. Her hands once more fell limp between her knees, her shoulders drooped as if she tired.

The spinning cone no longer kept its shape. Rather now it showed as a staff. Then it assumed vaguely humanoid form. At last there stood before the furred one a manikin, roughly formed, with but a ball for the head, the body closer to a collection of sticks. Still in the ball head opened pits and a slash—eyes and mouth.

Those eyes fastened on Malkin, the mouth writhed open. From it issued a twittering sound as high pitched as the squeak of a mouse. Then with a speed which sparked Thora's fear the stick legs pivoted and the creature whirled to face her.

She could not look away. The dark hole eyes caught and held her gaze with such strength that she clutched her moon gem the tighter. Deep in those pits was a projection of power—not Malkin's, the girl was certain. The furred one might have summoned this thing but she was not mistress of it.

The mouth opened and the squeak became speech:

"To the north—there is need—"

Thora marveled at the authority, the command in that whisper of a voice. This thing was only a projection—but the will behind it pierced through her own cherished independence to fasten upon her.

Then the manikin writhed, twisted. Thora shivered from a thrust of pain in her own body. One of Malkin's clawed hands swept out, two of the talons came together with a snap just above the head of the manikin who now wavered back and forth as if it were gripped by hands trying to wring out its life. Not from within this circle of safety did that attack come—no, the source lay outside—between what they saw and what had sent it forth.

Malkin's cutting brought an end. The manikin winked out of existence, while the furred one gave a cry and sank forward, face down on the cloak, one hand falling to rest above the

spiral and the other on the Moon Sign of the
Lady. Thora thrust her gem again into hiding
and went to her.

The furred one's body was limp, her eyes
closed. However even as Thora strove to
straighten her in support, those eyes opened
with a fierce blaze. Kort was on his feet,
growling deep. Above them oak branches
stirred, tossing as if assaulted by the beginning of a storm, save there was no wind, only a
spattering of acorns loosed to fall. Then the
trees stilled. Kort sat, though he continued to
hold his head high. Malkin turned a little in
Thora's hold.

"Ssssettt—" Her tongue fought for words
—"Nooo commmeee heerree— Ssssaffeee—"

Once more that feeling of safety was close
about them—warm, comforting—as if they
had been gathered tightly into a loving em-
brace. Yet Thora knew that the enemy had
tried to reach them.

"Weeee goooo—" Malkin continued,
"Maaakilll caallls—"

She did not try to shake off Thora's hold,
rather she rested against the girl as if she had
taken some wound from her own spelling.
Malkin must be suffering now from that
draining of inner power which she had expended in the making of the manikin.

Again the clawed hand moved as Malkin's
head rested against Thora—the wide mouth
opened and her breath came and went in small

panting gasps. The furred one waved weakly to one of the vials she had brought from the storage place. Snatching up the nearest the girl put that into the feeble hand.

Pushing free the cap, the other licked at the powder as Thora continued to support her. As a restorative the dust worked swiftly, the furred one sat erect on her own as she looked to the girl and nodded.

"Maaakilll livesss—" There was triumph in that. "Weèe gooo—"

Thora sat back on her heels. It was true that to her one place in this strange country might well be as good as another. Only in her stirred a small resentment. She was Mother Chosen—near to being a priestess. The man in her vision was greater than any Horned Priest—she sensed that. But his power was a contradiction of terms which she was not able to accept. The *Lady* wrought through her Daughters—theirs was the power. No priest could hope to call *Her* save through the Priestess. Yet the will she knew had animated that manikin for a space had in some way influenced her and that it was a man who had done this. There were many peoples in this land of which she knew little—look at Malkin whose like she had not dreamed would exist.

With those of Set it was the priest who was the vessel of power. Still this Makil was not of Set. What WAS he then—this one who wore a man's body and yet was able to call upon good? She shook her head at her own thoughts. In spite of that spark of resentment, she knew that she would indeed go north—into what danger she might not begin to reckon—whether she willed it or not.

While they spent the night within this forgotten sacred place, Kort went hunting. However, he did not bring a fresh kill for Malkin. Even that four-footed ranger accepted the age-old rule that fresh blood could not flow within a shrine. It was those of the Left Path, the Dark, who broke that Law. Their perverted followers slew even upon a very focus stone. Then even the true Power could not banish such shadows as lingered there to stain and destroy.

Malkin counted the vials left in her store —five. Of those she uncapped another and licked half its contents. Then she pulled the cloak straight, wrapped her supplies within it. Thora ate of her own meager rations.

She half expected that in this place she might meet with another vision. The spell casting should have alerted the force brooding here—old as that might be. For any arousing of a place of the Ancient Learning brought answers. She made a slow round of the circle, nothing but the moss grew within the circle of tree and stones.

The sweet scent of the tree embracing flowers gathered strength at the setting of the sun. Yet this night she dared not dance down power, for the Mother Lamp was not out and this was a time of full darkness. Still she was restless. Though Malkin had curled up, her head pillowed on the folded cloak, Thora had no wish to join her. Now came a sighing of wind through the trees. The girl listened—not knowing what she sought.

At last she came to the North Stone and there settled, her back against its strength, her hands upon the knife which she had driven point deep into the earth so the steel stood firmly balanced. As Malkin had done Thora hummed, but this was no conscious threading of one word to another to summon. Rather, she realized with a start, what she sang without true words was the sowing song—that spell of the Lady which her Chosen, be they already raised up priestesses or children hardly from the back cradle, sang as they walked together over the new-turned field, sowing afar the first Hand-take of seed. Yet there was no field here, her companions of the past were dead—if they were lucky. For the raiders were of the Dark, and any vowed to the Mother were among the first they would rape and slay.

No field for sowing—no. But the Lady's sowing could be for more than a stretch of plow turned ground. It could lie within a person—bringing a woman into fruitfulness. She sang the sowing and somehow that was right—though the Lady had not yet revealed to her why that should be so.

With the coming of full dark her song ended. Shadows drew in beneath the trees, yet with them they brought no fear. The stones stood as lamps though their radiance did not travel far. Thora watched Kort, back from his scouting, stretch out on the ground, to rest head upon paws. The perfume was ever stronger. One might be burying one's face in a load of flowers. She slipped farther down her rock support and slept.

In the morning the grove had lost some of its mystery. The Power had ebbed, or else withdrawn to be stored against some future need. There were only stones and trees with no protection to be felt.

The three went on, heading north. Though Malkin started off at a pace faster than any she had kept before, Thora knew the danger of becoming too fatigued and cut back their speed to that of the trail stride she had followed through months of roving. By mid-morning she brought down two of the large birds of the grassland, and, finding an overhang of river bank (for the country was growing more hilly with a smudge on the horizon to denote real heights beyond), she built a small fire to broil some of the meat. Malkin ate raw bits from the second carcass which she shared with Kort. They filled their water bottle and drank deep.

The river was shrinking. Perhaps those storms which had fed it at their coming had now subsided. Kort quested back and forth ahead. The sun was hot, the day warmer than usual. Malkin lagged and Thora called more rest halts now and then.

Kort came to a sudden pause. He did not bark, but rather turned his head and looked back at Thora, the whole stance of his body telling her this was something of importance. Nor did he return, but waited for them to join him.

There was a patch of clay here, softened by yesterday's rain. In it a sharp print. That was no animal spoor but rather the clear impression of a traveler's boot. Kort sniffed at it. However it was not the hound but Malkin who surprised Thora. The furred one knelt, her red eyes wide open. She, too, went down on all fours and her tongue flickered out, back and forth, not quite touching the print itself.

The furred one then took up the spear she still carried as a staff and, using its point, pricked the skin on her wrist. A drop of purplish blood gathered. Malkin dropped the spear, to squeeze before she held the wrist over the track so that blood fell in a thick blob into the center of the print.

For a moment or two it lay inert, as if the clay were too thick to absorb it. Then it spread outward, forming a circle. Malkin watched it so intently that she might be summoning up a second manikin. The circle put forth two horns, so well marked they could have been so shaped with a brush.

Malkin's breath came with a sharp hiss. She raised her wrist to her mouth and licked the cut, but her eyes never left the print and the blood.

"What do you do?" The girl could no longer contain her curiosity. There was hunting power, yes—she had seen such in action—had used a little of it when she must. Only this was plainly a ritual foreign to her own teaching.

Malkin raised her head, her eyes at full glow. "Isss oneee—whoooo issss—offf—"

Thora guessed by the horns— "Set?"

Malkin's head shake was violent. "Goooddd — offf — Maakill — Brotthher oneee—"

"One of his clan?"

Malkin nodded now. Thora looked at the splotch of blood. It had not yet sunk into the ground, but remained clear. However, the furred one raised her spear, and, with a quick, sure stroke, brought the butt down upon the blood spot, driving it so into the ground as to destroy it.

"Ggooo—" Malkin stood. She pointed to Kort and then to the defaced print, suggesting, Thora was sure, that the hound take up the trail.

One of Makil's kind then. Thora was not sure she was ready to meet him even if they did catch up. But it would seem she had no choice, for Kort, nose to the ground, loped steadily on. While Malkin limped in his wake at the best pace she could keep, and Thora was left for rearguard.

The sun was westering now. In this strange territory they should be seeking out some defensible shelter for the night. Still neither of her companions showed any sign that they intended to turn from the trail.

They were shut off on the east by steadily rising ground. The stream here ran in a more narrow and deeper channel between what were approaching cliffs. It would seem they had come near to the end of the open land. Scattered about grew a tangle of brush and small stands of trees. Thora could see ahead the line of what was a sizeable wood. Kort reached the edge of that and stood waiting for them.

The girl marked the mouth of a trail, wider, she decided, than a game one. She eyed that unhappily. If this was a path in use by men— she thought of the traders—however Kort had not warned them away, and she must be reassured by that.

Malkin appeared to have no uneasiness, and kept marching straight ahead. Now Kort trotted with her. The girl shifted her backpack. With spear in one hand and her other one hovering near the hilt of her knife she went forward into the cool of the wood, straining to hear. There were no oaks here, nor any wealth of flowers. She did see the hooks of uncoiling ferns and heard the sounds of birds, and once or twice a small rustling close to ground.

Then—

It was as if she had walked into a wall!

Thora staggered back, the force of meeting that invisible barrier near over balancing her. Malkin, Kort—they had met no such challenge. The girl put out both hands, half certain there was a hidden wall there.

Her fingers encountered no surface, it was just that they could not pierce beyond. She spread her hands wide, tried to push. There was nothing to feel. Simply that she could not pass—what—air itself? Malkin and the hound, were nearly out of sight.

She uttered a cry and Malkin wheeled to look back. Then, at a limping run, the furred one returned to where Thora stood, still striving to press her hands into the air. Malkin also put out a hand as if she sought what Thora fought against. Whether she guessed the nature of the barrier the girl could not tell, but she was back beside Thora, her eyes aflame.

"I cannot go on," the girl said. "There is a power set against me."

"Sssssoooo—" Malkin turned up the wrist from which she had earlier dropped the blood on the footprint. She looked from it to Thora.

"Bllooddd—" She drew the single word into a long hissing sound.

Once more she pricked at the cut, watched a bead of blood gather there. Then she held up her arm.

"Drrinnkk—"

Thora jerked back. Blood was life. Two men, two women could share blood, so giving and taking, and then be bound more tightly than any kin. If one shed blood for food, or in anger, one must follow ritual—or one lay under the Shadow. She looked at the welling bubble of dark blood and felt a little sick. Malkin's eyes blazed. She dropped the spear and clutched at the girl, striving to drag her down closer.

"Drrinnkkk—" That was a command.

Reluctantly, Thora inclined her head as Malkin thrust the bleeding wrist higher. She had to fight revulsion as she allowed her lips to open, to touch the other's fur-covered flesh. She sucked and the moisture she so drew in burnt her lips and her mouth like fire, but she swallowed, because at this moment Malkin's will subdued her own. Then she stepped forward. There was no wall holding her back now.

The path of the wood led steadily upward into broken country. For three days they followed it into sharp ridges and higher hills until it ended at last at the base of a rise Thora could see no way of climbing. Kort trotted eastward along the base of that cliff, nosing among the debris of earth and rocks, half embedding here and there the trunk of some long-dead tree, evidences of a mighty landslip. But Malkin stayed, looking up, her bushy head far back on her shoulders—not measuring the cliff Thora thought, rather searching the sky beyond.

Since the furred one had brought her past that invisible barrier, the girl had been uneasy. All the tests she herself knew confirmed that Malkin was not a follower of Set. Still, her powers were of a type unheard of among Thora's own people. And the unknown was always suspect—caution was the first weapon for those in unknown lands.

Now Malkin was singing again, but the sound was so low it was like a whisper. Though the singer still held her head at what must be a most uncomfortable angle, searching the sky. It was mid-morning and that spread of blue was cloudless, the heat of the sun reflected from the stones about them.

Out into that blue arch of sky came what was at first only a black mote, which could have been covered with a fingertip. The flyer grew larger, moving from side to side in long gliding sweeps, descending lower with each.

A bird? Thora was sure that outline against the sky was that of far outstretched wings. Only, even among the winged ones who rode the air currents thus, there must come a beat of wings now and then, and never did these change position. There was something wrong about the outline of the body those still wings supported—it looked far too slender—too small in proportion to the wings.

The creature of the air dipped closer and closer. Thora moved up beside Malkin, her arm touched the furred one, and she felt the rhythm pulsing through that smaller body, though her song was so muted.

Then the winged creature gave a sudden dip, sailing across where they stood, to vanish beyond the lip of the cliff before them. But it did not pass so soon from sight that Thora had not seen plainly what she would never have accepted for the truth had another reported it. The body stretched horizontally beneath those beatless wings was that of a man! By some art or power he was as free of the air above as if he had been born feathered!

Malkin now watched the top of the cliff over which the flyer had vanished. Kort sat on his haunches, his nose pointing in the same direction.

"Who—?" Thora found her voice and pointed, determined to catch Malkin's attention, learn what manner of man dared so use the sky.

The furred one without looking away from the cliff twisted her tongue to answer:

"Winnnd Ridder—Waiittt nooooww—"

Before Thora could ask for further enlightenment, something fell from the cliff top. She saw that straighten out into a dangle of thick ropes which swung back and forth.

There was a loop knotted at the end which had fallen almost directly before Malkin.

Without showing any surprise, the furred one picked that up, set the loop about her waist and pulled it snug. She made sure of the fastening of the rolled cloak, thrust her spear through the thongs securing that, and then gave a vigorous tug to the rope.

It was being pulled up, Malkin kicked out now and then against the wall, as if she had done this many times over. Thora watched her reach the top and vanish as the flyer had done. Once more the rope toppled over, to fall in coil. To follow Malkin so—but there was really very little choice. Kort had come forward stiff legged, as he always did when approaching that concerning which he was uneasy. He lowered his head, pushed his nose under the loop, then stepped forward so it was about his body, looking to Thora with an unmistakable command to make him fast.

With a kick or two—whoever was on the other end of that line must have sensed the dog was secure—Kort faced the wall of stone. He used his four feet to fend himself away, and up he went—to vanish with a flurry of paws.

6

Thora checked the security of her pack, thrust her spear into its sling, making sure it was well knotted. Once more the rope was tossed down. She heard Kort bark encouragingly. Trusting in him as she had so many times before, the girl steadied the loop about her, waiting for an upward pull which followed at once, though it seemed a long time until the edge of the rise was within reach. She pulled herself over, her scramble landing her near face down.

As she rose to her knees she viewed a very wide ledge of stone—stretching well out before her. However her attention was drawn to the man beside Malkin, the rope coils he was looping in. He was so tall Malkin seemed doubly dwarfed beside him, he must top Thora herself by a head, and she was well grown by the standards of her people.

His body was covered by a form-fitting suit of dull, dark green that revealed him as lean, long of limb, narrow of hip. Only his shoulders were wide and highly developed in proportion to the rest of him. His head was bare, and his hair so closely cut that it was like a tight black cap.

Like the rest of him, his face was long, thin of cheek, sharp of nose, pointed of chin. The exposed skin was dark brown, against which his large eyes (as brilliant as Malkin's, but green) and scarlet lips showed in bright color.

On the breast of his all-enveloping garment was a spiral emblem, a larger copy of that on the cloak, and that was wrought in the Lady's own precious silver. He continued to coil the rope, though his eyes were on Thora as if he discovered her as amazing a sight as she found him.

Behind, on the level rock of this wide shelf, rested the strange winged thing which had borne him, the same dark green as his clothing. Kort sniffed along the jutting tip of one pinion, as if to acquaint himself firmly with a new scent.

The stranger let fall his rope, now neatly packaged. He held up a hand palm out in the age old signal of peace and spoke:

"I am Martan, the Winged." A bald statement which Thora answered with the same brevity:

"I am Thora, the Chosen." She added the title since she was determined to be known at once as one of the Lady's own. She would not allow herself to remain a lesser person before this one, even if he possessed such skills as he had demonstrated.

But, as if he were dismissing her, he now extended his hand to Malkin, who seized upon it eagerly as she looked up into his face. She might have been making some unvoiced demand upon him.

He spoke again, this time directly to the furred one.

"All is well with Makil, little sister. He was wounded, but he mends and his mending will speed the sooner with his blood-one by him."

His seeming lack of further interest in her was an irritation to Thora.

"What are you—beside winged?" she demanded abruptly. "From what shrine do you draw such power? Who are your Three-In-One?"

A slight race of frown showed on his face. He stooped and caught up Malkin, who settled against him with a sigh as if at long last she had come home. Thora frowned in turn. Why did he act as if she were invisible—that the furred one was all important? No man had the right to so ignore a Chosen!

"You speak of things," he said deliberately,

"of which I do not know." His hand touched the spiral on his breast. "We have a source of power, yes. But one does not speak commonly of such."

That was a rebuke and she smarted under it. That *he* should undertake to lesson her in proper ways! Still, because it was never wise to carry strife into the unknown lest the enemy have hidden resources, she battened down her longed-for hot answer and spoke as deliberately as he:

"Other people, other customs. Where do you propose to take us Winged One?"

Now he studied her narrowly, as if he sensed her rebellion. Only he did not add to the insult he had already offered her. Rather he half turned, glancing over his shoulder to where Kort still sniffed along the wings.

"You cannot bear us hence with that!" Thora objected. Though she did not know the limits of his power, she, for one, would not go skimming off into the air with this stranger.

He smiled then, or at least his lips curved, even if the harsh green of his eyes did not lighten.

"I could not rise myself now—from here —one needs the upper peaks and the strong currents there to launch one. I was sentinel when the sister's heart-call reached me—thus I came." His arm about Malkin tightened, and, with his free hand, he smoothed the bushy hair back from her small face as tenderly as if he held a child of his own blood. "Those," with a lift of his chin he indicated the wings, "must remain here for a space. Our way now will be trod by foot alone."

Abruptly he turned and, at the same time, Kort left off his investigation of the flyer, came to the man as if he had been whistled at—a desertion which added to Thora's sense of outrage. As the stranger started away, with Kort at his heels and Malkin in his arms, she fell in behind, nursing rising anger but knowing she had no choice.

Though this country seemed wild and unsettled to the eye Thora discovered that that appearance was deceiving, perhaps one deliberately fostered. Her guide made a detour around a tall rock and before them arose a series of steps cut into the side of the next range of heights and leading upward, very plainly the work of men.

These the man climbed with a springing step, as if he was well at home on such a road. However Thora crowded close to the wall averting her eyes from the drop on her right. The climb was a long one and the heights towered well above the ledge on which the flyer now rested.

Here the air was chill. In some of those heights the snow must still lie on the ground. Though the steps were wide, but there were also longer spaces where one might pause to rest. Though, because their guide did not take advantage of these, Thora would not allow herself to lag behind. Her legs were beginning to ache with the strain of this endless climb.

It seemed that half the day had passed (though the girl knew that was not so) before they came out on another wide platform backed by a building which was part of the solid cliff itself. There was a doorway, deep incised over it the spiral symbol, narrow slits of windows flanking it—a row of those extending along one side until the cliff was beyond the ledge.

From the doorway stepped another man, dressed in the same close-fitting clothing. He was enough like Martan to have been his brother. Except that this newcomer had a frosting of gray across his cap of hair, Thora could hardly distinguish one from the other.

"Little sister!" He held out his arms to Malkin. The furred one made a crooning sound and went to him eagerly. Then there came trotting out of the door another of Malkin's own people, a male. Seeing her he raised his head, uttering a loud, hooting cry. Kort sat down to watch the scene as might a hound who had done his duty well and Thora longed to drop beside him. Only pride kept her on her feet, facing stiffly these men who were so lacking in proper respect that they did not know the deference due a Chosen.

For the first time Martan seemed to recall that she was a member of their party for he turned and waved her forward.

"This is Thora who has brought our sister!" He made introduction to the older man, though he did not carry through the courtesy and speak that one's name to the girl in turn.

A second pair of hard green eyes surveyed her. Then the older man nodded:

"Who has aided our sister, has aided us. Come—"

Her stiff pride got the better of her. Thora remained where she was and her voice rang out coldly, as if to lesson some stupid trader to a proper sense of what was correct.

"I am a Chosen, Man—" deliberately she used the bare word of address which could be one of scorn if a woman willed it so. "If you are not of the Dark—then you know the rule of the Lady. From my hands can come Her blessings—when She wills it!"

There was a shade of expression on his face which Thora could not interpret though she was sure it was not recognition of his own present discourtesy. Instead he uttered two words—though the accent he put upon them was unlike that which she had been taught. Yet they were part of an invocation of the Power. Swiftly she answered them, completing that fraction of ritual as might any one who could sing down the Moon.

Now he did register real surprise. Malkin moved in his hold, not striving to form words with her tongue, but uttering a series of hisses which the girl judged to be her normal speech pattern. He listened gravely and then spoke again:

"It seems that there are things to learn. Malkin tells me that you are one of the True Light and that you stand against the Dark even as we—though you work by a different pattern. To us all who do thus are welcome—and you doubly so for what you have done for our little sister. Also she tells me that you are now blood-bound to her."

Martan gave a start, staring at Thora. Before she could avoid him he took from her her pack. Then he offered his arm as if for her support, but she avoided him with a definite shake of her head.

They went into the cliff house past a cunningly devised barrier which Thora saw was faced with bits of stone fitted skillfully together, so that, when it was closed, it must resemble entirely the native rock. There ran a long corridor, crosswise lighted through the slit windows, yet still dusky. The inner side of that was broken by three doors of heavy wood and it was to the center one of those that the older man led them. Here was a room cut out of the rock, the walls of which were deeply incised with the spiral, and those incisions filled with colors, gold, green, blue—all well displayed by baskets of burning stuff fastened to those same walls.

On the floor were mats of heavy reeds and

the skins of the fabled mountain bears of which traders told horror tales—one of the most-to-be-feared predators of their world. There was furniture, plainly finished, with no touches of that ornamental carving which Thora's people favored. But the surfaces were polished and the chairs cushioned with pads made of reeds or cattle-hide quilted with thongs. On a long table, sided by benches, were dishes and another man moved quickly about, bringing goblets to set out along that board, plainly preparing for a meal.

Thora realized that she was not only hungry, but that it had been very long indeed since she had eaten. She sniffed the smell of roasting meat and freshly baked bread, such as she had not put tooth to since the Craigs had fallen. Now she had to summon up pride to keep her from an onslaught on that table and the filled trays the serving man was bringing from a curtained inner door.

All of these men were dressed alike. There appeared to be no insignia of different rank among them. The two serving the table had glanced up when the others entered and then away—as if to view strangers violated some rule. There were no signs of any woman's presence. Thora was disappointed. No matter how high these men might hold themselves, she was sure that any woman would recognize her at once as a Chosen—one to be held in esteem.

The man carrying Malkin placed the furred

one on a raised portion of bench so that she could see well above the top of the table, and the male of her species at once climbed up beside her, reaching out to touch her gently, then give a tug to the cloak she still carried. There were no dishes before her and she unrolled her burden to display those vials with their dust. As Malkin revealed these the man who had brought her in caught one up, to hold it closer to the nearest basket light.

"Where is this from?" There was urgency in his demand. Quickly he crossed to Thora holding out the vial almost accusingly. "Where did you find this?"

"Malkin found it," she retorted. "It was in a container in the underground place—"

"Underground place?" he seized upon that. The two men who had been bringing in the food stopped, stood still behind him. Martan loomed up by her side as if they would ring her in.

Thora refused to be overawed. Instead, speaking deliberately, she told her tale of how Kort had led them underground and what they had found there—including the party of the dead led by the red-cloaked man of Set. She had gained their complete attention now, and they heard her out to the end before their leader said:

"A place of storage—"

Martan broke in. "And one known to those of the Dark!"

"Maybe not at present," the older man returned. "If any escaped death they would not have left the body of their priest. Also," he turned again to Thora, "you said they were long dead, did you not?"

"Yes."

"So. Then that could even have happened in the Time of Wandering. If so, none of the Dark Followers would know of it now or it would be looted. What could lie there!" His hand tightened about the vial until Thora thought he might crush it. Then he turned and set it back among the others Malkin had put out. The furred one had forced the cap off one and handed it to her companion who licked up the dust with every appearance of satisfaction and pleasure.

"It was a pity that cloak was not destroyed," Martan commented. "Like calls to like—even after years—let one of the adepts approach near enough and it would draw him there."

"True," the elder took a quick stride and then came back. "You can find this place again?" he asked Thora sharply.

"If I could not, Kort can." She remembered their fight with the things of the dark cliff. "There are those there on guard," and she explained about their battle.

Martan nodded. "Yes, the rock rats. Such we have faced before. There are worse things to be met with when one walks in the ways of the Dark. Now—Lady, you are our guest and there is food waiting—"

He spoke with none of the sharpness which the leader had shown, his voice was low and pleasant as he indicated the table. Nor did the leader add any comment, but rather appeared lost in thought as he went to the other side of the board and seated himself. Martan sat beside Thora on one side, the two furred ones on her other. One of the serving men brought a larger platter piled high with meat which he put on the floor before Kort.

When they were all seated, the elder raised his hand and made the spiral sign and the rest of them followed his example, save that Thora spread her fingers in the salute to the Lady.

It seemed that here conversation during a meal was not the custom, for they sat in silence, helping themselves from platters set in the middle of the table. Thora broke her portion of fragrant new bread so that its crust served to sop up the rich gravy and she ate slowly, savoring the taste of the meat, the subtle seasonings. This was provender such as the Craigs had known only on feast days.

When they were done Martan arose with the other three, carrying away the platters. Malkin slipped down from her bench, going to the still-seated elder, raising hand to his sleeve. He started at her touch as if awakening from deep thought.

"Ah, yes—Makil. Very well, Malkin, you shall soon see him. Also," he glanced now at

Thora, "this is but an outpost of our land, Lady. There are those beyond who will be eager to hear what you have to tell us. There is trouble rising and he who goes forewarned, goes doubly armed."

But it would appear that their hospitality was offered for a night. Upon awakening early Thora sat on the edge of a shelf bed within a niche. They had primitive quarters, these cliff sentries. For the only softening of the stone under her was one of the reed mats, her trail pack had been her pillow. Now, having splashed in a stream of water piped through a runnel along the side of the cave-chamber, she twisted up her damp hair, fastened it with a worn thong. This looked more like the cell of a prisoner than a guesting place.

Was she a prisoner? She still had her weapons—nor had they searched her trail pack. Perhaps, she scowled, they believed themselves so armored against the power of hers that they need take no such precautions. The older man, whom she knew now as Teban, was very sure of himself.

She reached out a booted foot and toed Kort's ribs where the dog stretched upon the floor. The fact that this old companion had so manifestly welcomed the men was another blow to her self-esteem.

Kort lifted his head and Thora was promptly ashamed of her ill temper. Because she did not understand these people she had no right to

judge them. One learned in the ways of the
Mother must keep a serene mind, not nurse
small irritations. She stood up and Kort arose
with her, butting his head against her as he
had in the long ago days when he was still a
puppy and would so entice her into a game.
The girl fondled his ears, running her fingers
through his coarse fur.

"Who are these in truth, Kort?"

"We are men."

Thora whirled, her hand falling on the hilt of
her knife. Martan stood there, one hand on the
hide door curtain.

"Men lacking in courtesy." She showed
teeth as Kort might do. "Since it seems that
you move upon guests without doorward re-
quest." Had she been under observation?
Though she had seen no hole or crevice in
these rock walls to serve prying eyes.

She saw his lips twitch and then he answered:

"You do well to remind me, lady. When one
is on patrol one becomes accustomed to the
ruder ways of the garrison—"

Thora interrupted. "You make a mock of
me, man." She would not yield even the small
politeness of his name. "You call me 'lady'.
There is only ONE to be so called—and to use
Her name lightly is an insult. I am Chosen—if
you would bespeak me by other than my
name!"

He bowed his head a fraction. " 'Chosen' you

shall be then. I mean no insult to the Great Mother. Only, among us women are few, and those who share our lives are held in high honor. They do not venture forth from their homes for any save a very grave reason."

She thought his eyes flickered over her disparagingly—from her worn boots to her rough hair.

"It is not for any one to bide in soft shelter when there is life to be lived and duties to be done. If your people reckon thus—then I pity any woman born among you." Her chin lifted defiantly. "Nor does the Lady teach us so. *She*, in *Her* time, has gone against Set with sword in hand, the light of battle shining about *Her*. Thus also shall Her Chosen, and even those who are women-of-the-hearth, and mothers-of-all, take a stand when there is need. None of us must be protected." Thora near spat that word, so unpleasant did she find it. "Above all none who Moon Draw. The Hunter summons the men—*She* the women—in any battle we are as one!"

He had raised his hand to run his knuckles back and forth along his chin.

"Again I must plead that I meant no ill, Chosen. It would seem that though we walk in the same direction, our paths are separate. Bear with us since there is real danger and perhaps you shall find your battle sooner than you think. We break our morning fast now, and then we shall be on the road. Malkin pines for her blood-brother and he will, in turn, heal the faster when he knows the little one is alive and well."

There were only three of them at the table this morning—Malkin, Martan, and she. The furred one did not eat from one of the vials, rather she cupped between her handles a goblet in which a thick scarlet liquid arose to the brim. Blood! And Malkin drank it greedily as one long denied a special food. Resolutely Thora tried to accept such a diet as ordinary.

Luckily the cakes and dried fruit on her own plate were enough like the usual fare of the Craigs that she could consume them. She found the bread well flavored and drank with appreciation the cider in a mug Martan handed her—its tang warning her it was a more powerful beverage than it might appear.

Teban did not come to say farewell nor was there any sight of the other. They might well now have the outpost to themselves. Once fed, her pack again on her shoulders, Thora was ready to go. Martan picked up Malkin and together they went down another narrow corridor coming once more into the open.

There was a trail as clearly marked as the roads pounded by the traders in the lower lands. The way was narrow but deeply cut, as if years of constant use had sunk it below the surface of the surrounding rock. Sometimes the track ran dizzily on the very edge of drops where Thora longed to close her eyes, then, again, it climbed as steps or crossed open plateaus.

At intervals were narrow stretches where it was necessary to set one foot almost directly before the other in order to proceed. Then would stand towers of stone, or else doors and narrow loopholes cut in the rock walls, as if these were points fashioned for easy defense against any invader.

Thora saw no guardians at any such point, but she felt herself under observation as they passed. What these height dwellers guarded themselves so against she could not guess. Surely not any beasts—the enemies must be men. And for a very long time, judging by all she saw, that enmity had continued. The homestead of the Craigs had never been so protected. Perhaps had her own people been more menaced and had had to live under fear, the Craigs would have survived the raiders.

By noon they had won to a much higher point. Twice during their journey Thora sighted a winged one riding air currents aloft. Martan called a halt at a spot where a number of tall, fang-shaped rocks were set in a cluster, and, into the heart of these he guided them.

There had been no talk among them as they journeyed. Thora was too filled by a growing resentment against these people, while Martan wore constantly a preoccupied look as if his mind was well removed from what they did. Now it was as if he shook himself free

from some burden he had carried all morning.
He smiled at her, seeming much younger,
more akin to her own kind. Thora knew she
must not betray any petulance, that showing
such here and now would be akin to the
pouting of a child who wished only her own
way. She must meet any overture which he
might make so to learn more—much more
—concerning all these spiral wearers and
their ways.

7

"Do you live here, Windrider—where even in summer there must lie some snow among the peaks?" she asked, as she took supplies from her backpack, offering a twist of meat to Kort. She had been handed a bag of trail rations that morning, to find such provided not unlike what she had been used to.

"Not here, Chosen." Martan munched on a round of bread spread with a thick yellow paste. "We are not too far from the Valley's entrance. To reach that we must descend a little. Our land is far from being as grim as what you see about you here."

"Have your people always lived here?" She did not know if these questions would be considered seemly, but she determined still to learn all she could.

"For a long time. Some of us came into shelter during the Days of Upheaval. A few had already found this place. It is a fertile land, our valley, and our numbers are such that there is room for all."

Now came the question which had been with her all morning:

"Who is your enemy, Windrider? This trail we follow is one clearly planned for easy defense."

She waited for a frown, perhaps even a rebuke for her curiosity. But his expression remained mildly friendly.

"The enemy has worn several faces through the years. Or perhaps all those were only masks, and that which was behind them was in truth always the same. The latter has come to be the belief of many of us. But these days it is the men of Set, openly so, and those who are their slaves or sworn servants."

Thora remembered the body taken from the river. Yes, Set was plainly abroad in the low lands. Then a thought flashed across her mind—those pirates whose raids had grown very much worse through the years—were they more than just wild men intent on pillage? Could they also be servants of Set working with a planned purpose?

"Servants and slaves," she repeated. "There are many of those?"

"Their numbers grow," Martan returned as

he´ chose a handful of dried berries. Malkin sheltered beside him, in her hand one of the vials. The furred one seemed intent on her feeding, paying them no heed.

"So you have been long at war—"

"Not at war if you mean large numbers of men engaged in open struggle. But we live with our eyes ready to spy the coming of the Dark. From time to time that laps up, to try and drag us down. Save that it never has succeeded. Still we are none the less vigilant because of that. Now—" he hesitated, "yes, the danger is increasing. Our people have been ruthlessly attacked several times on the plains. So far there has come no strike at even our outer ring of defense. But what we have learned argues that there is a new rise of Power among the Dark ones—and that they prepare to seek a goal. It may well be our valley or it may be something of which we are still ignorant."

"Your people not only man these hills but also go out into the lowlands?"

He hesitated so long she felt rebuffed. Then he spoke:

"I do not know the extent of your Before Knowledge, Chosen. Do your people seek out places of the Former Ones to learn their secrets?"

Thora shook her head vigorously. "That is forbidden. Once—in the far past—it was tried. Those who did so died, and also the people to

whom they brought their findings. There was
such a sickness that not even the Three-In-One
could heal. It ate up four clans before we fled
to live afar from such a cursed place. The Lady
gives us the knowledge we need, we do not
turn back to the ways of the past."

"Yes, there are places where it is death to
venture. But some of the old sites are clean,
and from those we have discovered much. The
wings on which we ride the winds come from a
place which one of our hunters found—and
there are other marvels. You, yourself, traveled through a storehouse. There were dead
there, but that death struck long ago. Perhaps
there lies that which would benefit us all."

Thora's fingers crooked in the warding-off
sign. She had not thought of this before. Had
she indeed broken the Law when she entered
that storehouse under the earth? But—it was
afterwards that she had found that forgotten
shrine. The Power lingering there had not
struck her down as if she had broken the
Word, or stood against the Lady. She drew a
deep breath. Even the thought of what she
might have done unwittingly was daunting.

"We have come to seek such secrets, both
for ourselves," Martan continued, "and because those of Set seek them also and they
must not gain knowledge which will allow
them to rise and sweep us and that which we
serve," his hand touched the spiral on his
breast, "wholly out of the world. It is on these

expeditions of discovery that our people have come up against Dark Ones who are ever on the move, sniffing across the land, even as your good hound here goes guesting. Makil was on the track of a great discovery when he was attacked by the Dark Ones who used a new weapon of which we must learn more.

"And you, Chosen, what brought you into this country which must be well away from your own, since our paths have not crossed before?"

"No searching for secrets, Windrider. I came because men of blood and war along the coast have taken now to haunt inland rivers." She told him a few stark words of the fall of the Craigs and of why she had drifted west.

Martan listened with close attention. "It would seem that those who follow the ways of death are on the march in all places—"

She spoke aloud her thoughts of moments earlier. "Then perhaps our raid is another work of Set's own, not just that wild men move as they did the early days Afterward. Yet we have never heard of any priest among them."

"It is not the priests who lead the van, rather their servants who are sent to prepare the way. Then when the land is ravaged and all resistance broken, the red cloaks show themselves. So have they worked in *our* past, so may they be working elsewhere. If this is so—"
He frowned now and his fingers traced the spiral, following the line about and about to its

center, "perhaps the evil is far more widely spread, the menace behind it greater than we have dreamed!"

A picture grew in her mind, summoned by his words. She seemed to be looking down upon a vast web being spun by a bloated bodied spider, the strands a foul black, crossing and recrossing, reaching out ever farther to shadow more of the clean earth.

"What can you do?" she challenged him. "Are there so many fighting men in this valley of yours, or are they so powerful, that they can rise up and push those of Set into the outer darkness forever?"

"Not so many, not so mighty—yet!" he answered her openly. "Still we learn, and, learning, we are better armed. And being better armed, we can indeed match evil where it springs. But two things you have brought, Chosen, which are of great value—first, news of the storage place of which we had only the vaguest hint that, it might exist somewhere. Second that your own people have fallen, and with them perhaps others along our borders, giving free passage to those, who if they are not already Set's agents, can speedily become so. This is indeed a time when there is open trouble and we must stir, lest we be swept away before we can rise to fight at all!"

He stowed away the remnants of his meal. Malkin was already on her feet, adjusting the cloak roll. Kort pushed out from among the stones. Thora stood up, swung her pack into its familiar position, checking as she always did the lashings of her throwing spear, the easy slide of her knife in its sheath.

They were faced by a stepped climb, sharper than any they had elsewhere fronted. On either side were twin towers from which men, in the same clothing Martan wore, emerged to view them, and then raised hands to wave them on.

At the top of that rise they issued out upon a platform—long and narrow—which extended for a long distance. Below them lay such a land as Thora had never seen. The far wall of it was far away enough so to be dim to the eyes, but she guessed from what she could perceive that she stood on the edge of a vast hollow— sharply sloping downward at first, then leveling out more where there were the green of fields. Its heart cupped a lake, from this distance as blue as the sky above, and, clustered to one side of that, what could only be dwellings.

White dots which must be sheep grazing were visible in the meadow land, and, beyond, the dun, or black and white of cattle. Small groves of trees spotted the countryside and there was the brown of fresh turned earth newly sowed. The far side of the lake was difficult to distinguish. The very size of this cup among the heights awed Thora. Indeed, with its wall so guarded, this could be a long-held place of safety. Martan had lingered, as if to give her a chance to see the extent of his land, but now Malkin hissed and he nodded.

"So be it, sister-blood. Yes, we go to Makil." He strode to the opposite side of the platform where there was the beginning of another stairway, and down they went, Kort, with a burst of speed, bounding ahead as if he were so wearied of rock that he could not wait to get good earth beneath his paws.

There came an end to the stair at last and Thora heard Kort bark, saw a party coming up a path to meet them. There were two men who might again be Martan's brothers, save they did not wear the form-fitting garment of the cliff sentinels, but rather more comfortable breeches and sleeveless jerkins which left their muscular arms bare and were akin to her own trail garments, except that on the breast of both jerkins the silver spiral appeared. They led a pony with a clipped mane and a well-curried coat, which tossed its head with a snort as it came to face Kort.

Malkin, whom Martan had carried down the stairs as he had carried her through most of the journey, slid down and ran, limping, to the pony which lowered its head to nose her with a force near strong enough to knock her off her unsteady feet. She raised both hands to catch at its cropped mane and so scrambled aloft, to seat herself firmly on its back, keeping her mane grip. Leaning forward she hissed into the animal's ear and it nickered, whisking about as one of the men loosed its halter, taking off at a rocking gallop down the slope.

Martan laughed and one of the men echoed him.

"The sister-blood is impatient. But Makil is no better—he made them bring him to a window seat even before the sun was high—when the message came. A good ending for both of them—this time—"

His companion nodded. "Far better than Makil dared hope. He has had the Loss Pain these many days and it was that which kept him to his bed, more than his wound. Now he will mend."

Thora saw their eyes stray in her direction, but it would seem that she still remained officially invisible. Or so it was until Martan said:

"This is Thora who is named Chosen among her people. It was she who aided the sister-blood."

Each of the men bowed his head to her, one saying "Dred" and the other "Jon," which she took to be their names, though they added nothing of kin nor clan to that.

"This is Kort." The girl laid her hand on the hound's head. "He is a great hunter and follower of trails."

As gravely as they had bowed to her, so did they also salute the hound before they moved down path. Malkin was already a very small figure far ahead, for, as one advanced on into the valley, that spread out much larger than it had looked from above. Thora saw that as the sun descended behind the height, lights were showing in the lakeside village.

She was tired and would be glad for shelter, but her pride would not allow her to express her need. Instead she matched her escort stride for stride, though she paid less heed to the short bursts of talk among them. Most of that dealt with matters of the valley—the health or presence of this or that person— some mention of a Uniting, which, she gathered, was a wedding. That brought an exclamation of surprise from Martan, a chuckle from Jon.

"Yes, Windrider. The Lady Alvas smiled upon Peet at last. He is now cloudminded, and we do not expect any good sense from him until the end of the Flower Moon. It is good fortune, for he was near the second name time, and, had she not spoken soon, it would have been too late for him."

"So it must be where there is only one lady and five or more ready to pay her court," observed Dred. "It has been hard for him these past days—"

Five men to a woman? Thora was surprised at that scrap of information. In the Craigs the ratio was very different—so much so that if a maid was not Chosen she went into some house-room as a second, or even a third wife. For it was necessary that there be children to serve the Lady. Had she herself not been born marked these three years past she must have selected the house-husband she wished and been a sharer in his home. For so long she had been glad she was born Chosen and had escaped the Law of Hearth Choice.

It was darker than twilight when they reached the village, coming to a house which sat in a garden of sweet smelling herbs already well above ground. The door was wide open, with lamplight fanning out to welcome them. Dred and Jon spoke farewells and went on, but Martan motioned Thora to that doorway. As they approached it there came one to stand waiting them there. He rested one hand on a furred shoulder while Malkin appeared to brace herself to support a burden. There was enough side light to show his face in part and Thora was not surprised that this was the man of her vision, he who had used the sword light against the Dark.

She surveyed him warily. The stranger now was urged back to a waiting chair by Martan, Malkin promptly settled herself in his lap, pulling his arm about her. His face was gaunt and carried lines set there by pain, but it was still young.

He wore a loose robe as might be for the bed-chamber, belted about him by a sash—but still with the silver spiral on the breast. His eyes were brilliant, seeming to glow as did Malkin's. Now he spoke polite words of welcome to Thora, and, more quickly, thanks for her aid to his familiar.

The girl was offered another chair, one of age-darkened wood, well cushioned, carved with the spiral. But she had hardly time to seat herself before the hide curtain to an inner room was lifted and a woman came in. Martan bowed low, but when Makil made as if to rise, the woman waved a hand. Her attention was fixed on Thora, and the girl, who had been on the point of getting to her feet in common courtesy, remained where she was, her chin high, her eyes meeting that cold gaze squarely and with a rising challenge she did not yet understand.

This female of the mountain valley could not be many years older than herself. But Thora saw her bleakly as one who wore a mask beneath which lay no liking for the Chosen. She was—soft—

Thora chose that word scornfully. The slender body was curved voluptuously here and there, her hands small, white, the feet in the ornamented sandals had never trod any trail. Her robe seemed to consist mainly of a number of nearly transparent strips or scarfs, rainbow colored and caught on her white shoulders with brooches which gave forth the glint of gems. Beneath her thrusting breasts the flowing garment was drawn in by a tight mesh belt in which more gems were set. The robe strips floated out freely as she moved, splitting now and then to show her ivory skin provocatively.

Her face was round, with a dimpled chin under a mouth pursed into a tight bud of deep pink, her nose slightly turned up at the tip. While her eyes were as brilliantly green as those of the men, her hair was not trimmed into the skull-tight cap, but hung long and loose. It was not entirely black either. Some strands were dark blue, others silver white—artificially colored, Thora guessed. There was a jeweled band across the top of the woman's head confining the locks to the back, and from that a second band protruded forward, dangling a small cluster of metal bells just above the forehead, bells which matched others edging the belt she wore. It was the strangest clothing Thora had ever seen, and one she found vaguely disturbing, for it emphasized so plainly the body of she who wore it.

More bells braceleted the wrists of the woman, and these rang as she held out both hands to Martan, he advancing eagerly to take what Thora decided were disgracefully soft and ineffectual fingers into his.

"My lady!" he bowed over those hands.

Thora stiffened more. To give that sacred title to this house dweller was a profanation. She felt blood rise warm in her cheeks as she longed to burst out with words which she had prudence enough to realize that she must not say. Other places—other customs.

"My lady," he repeated almost caressing-
ly—as if the female in her veils and jewels was
as important as a Chosen! "Good fortune to
this house, and to its mistress. You are gra-
cious to welcome us yourself."

The woman's lips arched in a smile Thora
read as superior. There was even a faint lisp in
the voice answering Martan:

"Always are you welcome, Windrider. Even
as our brother is—" She half withdrew her
hands from his hold and inclined her head towards Makil. Now she turned about again, setting all her bells tinkling, to face Thora.
Though she still smiled there was little
warmth in that stretch of the lips.

"You bring a guest, Martan—"

He started, flushed as might a child called to
order. That, too, Thora found distasteful.
There were currents of feeling here which she
sensed but did not understand. The open manners of her own people were familiar—here
she had no straight trail to follow.

"Lady," he was looking at Thora and she believed he might be comparing all the ways in
which she was unlike the valley female whom
he so plainly admired, "This is Thora, the
Chosen. She is from the east, of another people, but one who saved our sister-blood—thus
having claim on us."

"Thora," the woman inclined her head a
bare fraction. The green eyes measured,

probed. Thora blanked her face to meet this subtle assault. "And what may 'Chosen' mean, Thora?"

The girl leaned back in her chair, allowing herself a small smile in return, a stretch of lips as meaningless as that of the other.

"I serve the Three-In-One, born with the Lady's sign," she returned. Now she looked to Martan. "What name does this—this house-ruler bear?"

Two could play the game of making Martan remember that manners were manners. She was glad to see him redden once more.

"This is the Lady Sara," he said shortly, and she detected a flash of anger in his voice.

Thora raised a brown, briar scratched hand. At least her stubby nails were clean. She sketched the sign that the Chosen might use to a trader's woman, a subtle insult which this other might not recognize.

"May *Her* bounty serve this roof, house-ruler," she intoned as if she were one truly initiate. Nor did she believe that the Lady Herself would have found such pride ill in her. For the Mother was jealous for her servants—and surely this one could not draw down any power.

Sara had continued to smile, now she also added a graceful inclination of her head.

"Your fair wishing is kind, Chosen. I see you must have been many days roaming." That edged glance swept swiftly across Thora.

"Therefore let me take you into the inner chamber for refreshment."

Thora arose, caught up her backpack. "Well offered, houseruler," she returned brusquely. Kort moved over to her and the woman stared at him.

"There is a place outside for animals—" she began.

Thora interrupted. "We two are trail comrades, houseruler. Kort sleeps guardian for me, and I am ready to raise weapon," she touched her slinged spear, "for him. Perhaps it is not so among your people. But in this matter I must abide by the custom of mine."

That was a challenge and Sara recognized it, Thora was sure. The valley woman did not rise to it, but still smiled as she said:

"Let the hound accompany you then, Chosen. There are all too few good friends in this world for us to forget any. Come now, there will be rest and refreshment for the both of you."

Thora was reluctant. She knew too little of these people, and while it was true that the traveler must fit himself as well as he might (without betraying his true beliefs) to the customs of others there was something here which made her distrust being drawn into close contact with the valley woman.

Yet there was no other way. She raised her hand in trail salute to Martan who watched her with an odd shadow on his face, nodded to

Makil, who still held Malkin, and followed the
soft woman behind the curtain.

They crossed a second room, where there
was a table on which a servant was setting
forth food, and passed behind a carved screen,
Thora going ever more reluctantly.

On the other side of the screen the girl found
herself in another world—one which bore no
resemblance to any quarters she had known.
Traders had sometimes brought scraps of
fine, soft weaving from the south—but such
were not in full favor with the Craig people.
They preferred their own wool and linens,
their supple and well-cured leathers. Thora
had worked in the fashioning of all three into
garments, hangings, bedcovers. Here however
were drifts along the walls of the same sheer
stuff which failed completely to cover the
body of her hostess.

Also the girl's nose was assaulted by many
scents. The whole room seemed to be the same
pearl pink as the inside of a shell from the distant sea—and that pink steeped in perfume.

There was no closet bed such as was common in the Craigs—possessing sliding doors to
shut out the room if one would be private. Instead a mound of cushions, some the same
pink of the walls, some a deeper rose, one or
two, in contrast, bright blue-green, were piled
on a long ledge along the far wall. Flanking
that ledge were several small, stub-legged
tables, so that those who used them must

squat on the cushions. Some of these bore
vases with a spray or two of flowering branch,
on others were boxes of metal or clay painted
in bright colors. A mirror of polished metal set
on a rod so it could be held in the hand lay on
the nearest of those tables, beside it a dish
from which curled a thin trail of scented
smoke.

On the floor were deep-furred animal
skins—but not left in their natural colors. Instead they were dyed deep rose or bleached
white, while everywhere were piles of mats.
On two such sat other occupants of this room
who turned startled faces to the newcomers.
They were very young girls, hardly past child-
hood. Their plump bodies were clothed in sim-
ple white sheaths belted by cords, and they
had none of the belled jewelry which Sara
wore. Both of them rose quickly, their mouths
O's of astonishment as they stared at Thora
and Kort.

8

"This is Elsana, Dorotra—" Sara nodded in the direction of the girls. "Now, Chosen—"

But Thora's eyes had lighted on something which, for the first time, gave her a small feeling of security. The far wall was hung with a single long strip of cloth, and on that was stitched, by the finest of needlework, the orb of the Mother surmounted by the Crescent of the Maid. Thora's hand at once sketched the proper salute of reverence. Then she looked at Sara with a slightly different feeling. Though this woman might wear such clothing as seemed hardly decent to Thora, and though she dared to take to herself that title which was *Hers* alone among the believers, still Sara paid this much homage to the true faith. Now

Thora herself spoke the word which was that of greeting from one Moon server to another.

Sara's large eyes narrowed and her smile was gone. When she spoke her voice was cold, no longer so soft.

"That is no longer our way, Chosen. Long ago we made another choice."

Thora stiffened once more. "You may not recognize the greeting of the Mother, you may have no Three-In-One—yet there—" she pointed to the wall, "is *Her* own sign!"

Sara glanced from Thora to the two girls. "That Sign is an old one, we still pay it honor. But we have our own way. You speak of yourself as 'Chosen'—that once meant one of the Grove—"

"Grove?" Thora repeated. "I am one with those who draw the Moon—though I was not yet brought to *Her* as one of the Three. Our Maid, Matron, Elder, still held full power and it was not time for them to relinquish it. But I bear the Sign on my flesh and have since birth. Thus I was of Her House and of no homestead."

Sara looked puzzled. "It seems indeed that we speak of different things. But this is no time for such talk. You are our guest and you are weary, hungry. You shall be cared for—"

She must have made a gesture of which Thora had not been aware, for now the two girls closed in on either side. Her backpack was swept out of her hold, her weapon's sling with it. Before she had time to protest she was urged through another doorway into a bathing place where there was a basin in which waters washed sunken in the floor. One of the girls kilted up her short skirt, stepped quickly down to plug up both entrance and exit of a stream, while the other dived into a woven basket chest to bring out towels which she dropped nearby and then scurried off—to return with a pot of perfumed soft soap.

Thora shed her trail-worn clothes unhappily—wishing that she was to enter instead some woods pond. Free of her leathers and the linen body drawers and shirt she wore beneath (and which now shamed her by their soil), she stepped down into the bath. To her surprise the water was warm, as if that flow which had filled the basin had come straight from heating pots. She seated herself and proceeded to wash with vigor. Her hair she lathered, rinsed, and lathered again. Against the skin of her body her hands and arms looked very dark, as must her face—sun browned and wind burned.

Sara was gone, and, when Thora arose, Elsana had also gathered together the girl's discarded clothing and disappeared before she could protest. She was left with Dorotra. The younger girl, as Thora accepted the towel she held out, stared at the silver chain with the dangling moon gem.

"What is that?" she asked with the frankness of a child as Thora vigorously rubbed her hair. "Why do you wear it so?"

She could not take offense at such ignorance. It was plain that the child meant no harm, though among her own people any one hardly past the crawling stage would have known a priestess's girdle and been awed by the sight of it. Thora dropped the towel and cupped the gem in her hand as she would do to draw strength from it.

"It is the jewel of those drawing Moon power."

"Drawing power? But why do *you* wear it? You are a woman."

Thora caught her breath. Indeed these people must have strayed far from the true path if any could ask that question. Only among those lost to the truth was there ever any doubt of fact that the Lady worked only through the Three-In-One. The Hunter might come to the altar in his own time, but only a daughter could call the true power.

"Only a woman may call *Her*, do you not know that?" She must have spoken more sharply than she had intended, for the girl took a step or so backward, and looked frightened.

"You speak of things I do not understand, Lady—"

Thora's frustration forced her to answer that with nearly the same sharpness:

"There is only one *Lady*—none else may use

Her title. There are the Three-In-One—the
Maid, the Matron, the Elder. There are the
Chosen, who will in proper time, take their
places." She let fall the gem she had hand
warmed, and raised her right hand to point to
the mark on her breast. "Those who serve *Her*
directly are marked thus while still they lie
within the womb. Then there are Singers of
Power who raise voices sweetly, also by Her
gift—all these are women—but there is only
one *Lady!*"

Elsana backed another step, shaking her
head slowly from side to side. "Never have I
heard of any of these, Lad—Chosen. Your people must be very different—"

Suddenly Thora saw a chance to learn more
about the valley people. She tossed back her
damp hair and wrapped the largest of the towels about her, sitting on a small stool Elsana
had drawn forward. She smiled at the girl as
warmly as she could.

"Yes, it would seem that we are different.
Now I would learn how different. Tell me of
your people, Elsana. If they do not call down
power from the Lady through her Chosen—
how can they live? For I am sure that they *do*
follow the Path of Light."

Elsana spoke slowly at first, but, as Thora
continued to smile, asking a question now and
then, the younger girl gained spirit and at last
spoke freely. There was indeed a difference
here. As Martan had said, women were few

and very highly prized, so much so that they were virtually prisoners within their homes and never went out of the valley at all. Though within the dwellings they were completely deferred to.

There were many men with no wives. A "uniting" was a temporary matter at the whim of the woman, and in her lifetime she might have a number of mates. In the ratio of births it was one female to five males and all of those did not reach womanhood. The ritual of worship lay in the hands of the Elders—three men. The women had no true bond with *Her*, but they held their house power jealously. There were, Thora sensed quickly, intrigues and struggles within inner chambers of which perhaps the men were never aware.

Men were allowed only a certain number of years in which they could hope to attract the interest of any "lady." Then those considered past their prime for breeding strong children were given a "second name" and went to man the defense posts or become explorers who ventured into the outside world. The population within the valley was never very large and many of the males were away for long periods of time.

All learning and "remembering" was in the control of certain women—unless that dealt with war. Such a subject was treated with contempt and left to the men.

The more she heard the less Thora believed

that she could fit anywhere into the valley life. It would be better for her to go on her wandering way, out of such a closed world, back on the trail once again with Kort.

As if he had caught her thought, she now heard the dog she had left in the outer room bark and she arose—wondering where Dorotra had taken her clothes. That girl returned even as Thora gave a last rub to her hair, carrying in her arms a fluttering pile of colored drapery. Thora surveyed that before shaking her head firmly.

"My pack—" Winding a towel about her, she pushed into the other room to open the bundle, shaking out its contents. There was indeed a clean shirt and underdrawers, wrinkled, but smelling of the sweet bits of herb she had twisted into them. She pulled these on and then ordered Dorotra.

"Bring my clothes!"

"These—lady—" the maid held out the fripperies she carried.

Thora shook her head. "I wear only what is mine, girl. These are no proper robing for a Chosen." She flipped a finger disdainfully and a long streamer went fluttering through the air.

Dorotra looked to Elsana, back at Thora, and then turned to go. As she vanished, Thora spoke once more to the younger girl:

"You have spoken of your "ladies," but who are the furred ones—much as Malkin—and what part do these play in your lives?"

"They are the blood-kin—" Elsana looked more and more uncomfortable. "There are some men who can make blood-bond with them—then they are closer than a brother or a sister. For they take into them the man's blood, and he takes theirs—so they think with one mind and are never at fault with one another. When one dies the other deeply grieves—and sometimes the one left follows to death. I have seen it so.

"When a boy becomes a full man, he goes to the Forest and calls. If there is one among the Kin who is drawn to him in spirit that one comes. They drink each other's blood from that day forth, for, once bonded, the forest people depend upon blood for their life. Then those two are as one—tied together."

"But they do not ever come to a woman?"

Elsana looked shocked. "No! It is not fit— They choose only men, for us they do not care," her voice dropped to hardly above a whisper. "There was Hilba who would have a blood-sister and she went forth secretly. But our people found her wandering days later, and she was sick a long time. Thereafter she would never say what had happened. It may be the blood is a poison when it is drunk by a woman—"

Thora remembered Malkin's blood which had burned in her mouth, but had made her free of whatever barrier had closed the wood path. Certainly the burning might have made one believe it poisonous. But she had no ill effect.

"How—" she was beginning when Dorotra returned. Behind her was Sara. The woman was plainly not in the best of tempers.

"Is it right, Chosen, that you asked for these?" she indicated the leather breeches, jerkin, and boots which the maid carried. "Surely Dorotra must have been mistaken—"

Thora stood up. "Not so, householder. I asked for my proper clothing. I am not used to such splendors as you wear." She was willing in so much to placate the other. "Among my people I am a ranger of woodlands, for so is *She* when *She* chooses, knowing the bear, the wolf, the stag—calling upon them when *She* would go to battle. I have spent my time of training in the wilds and, since my people are now gone, I would remain still as I am, not losing my heritage."

"I do not understand you. But guests are not to be denied their desires. If it will suit you to do so—" Sara flung up her hands in irritated dismissal. "When you are dressed we have food—" She turned abruptly and went, leaving behind a firm impression that Thora was an awkward burden which must be borne.

For a moment the girl was abashed. Had she indeed offended against courtesy? But no, she could not yield to these valley ways. There was a stubborn core within her which made her feel that even to submit a fraction would lessen what the Lady intended her to be.

Dorotra had flounced off after Sara, the rejected robe bundled up under one arm. But Elsana remained, watching Thora draw on leggings and boots, latch jerkin over shirt, make sure the belt was securely buckled, that her knife rode easy on her hip.

"I do not understand—" said the valley girl in a half whisper—"is it with you that women are as the Windriders, the swordhanded? What are you, man or woman? For you have the body of one and you act as the other. It is not proper—"

She backed away as Kort arose to rub his head against Thora.

"There are many 'rights'," Thora replied. "Some exist for your people, some for mine. The rights do not matter, it is important that we face the same wrongs. Your guards have told me that you war with Set. Him also do all who serve the Lady call enemy. Therefore, after a fashion, we can be battle comrades—if not kin-friends."

Never in her far wanderings had Thora felt as alone as she did now, even though she was surrounded by those who wore the semblance of her own kind. She ate quickly and in silence of what Elsana put out on one of the small tables. Nor did she attempt any more conversation with the girl who had dropped down on a cushion some distance continuing to watch her closely. In her own mind Thora was trying to sort out her impressions, make some plan for the future.

That she would remain here in this peaceful yet alien valley—No! There was too much wary restlessness in her. Better to be away—on her own—seeking to answer that nebulous compulsion which had plucked at the edge of her consciousness for days. That she was part of some pattern she no longer doubted, but the manner of the weaving—no, it was not to be found here.

Sara did not return. When Thora had finished the food—well cooked, more tempting then she had eaten in months—she looked to Elsana.

"Who is your chief speaker? If you do not own the rule of Three-In-One, then whose orders carry weight?"

"There are the Silent Ones—" Elsana seemed confused. "But they do not rule within the household. They give orders for the Windriders—the outgoers—"

"They are men," Thora finished for her sharply. "Very well, I would speak with those who give orders. This is not my place—I do not abide with you—therefore I would go to seek my own way."

Fatigue weighed upon her. Inwardly she wanted nothing more than to curl up among these cushions and seek sleep. Still she distrusted this scented room which was so disturbing. Let her go with Kort—camp out in the meadow lands as she had done for so long.

Arising, she reached for the pack which she had laid to hand, and made sure her weapon sling was adjusted. Elsana, hand to mouth, watched her with troubled eyes.

"But—you must rest—this—" she waved at the room about them, "is for your guesting—"

Thora shook her head resolutely. She motioned to Kort.

"I am not of your people, your ways are not mine. I do not think that your mistress and I can deal well together."

Before the girl could answer, Thora turned and pushed past the screen—making for the outer chamber of the house. She heard a low murmur of voices and then she was into the lamplight of that first chamber. On the matted floors her hide boots made little sound. She had been so accustomed to walking with care that she was well into the room before Makil paused in mid-word to stare at her.

Malkin was still curled against him, by the look of her in deep sleep. His face was drawn into harsh lines but there was still about him an air of determination and purpose. Martan was gone, but a much older man leaned forward in a second chair, his closed fists on his knees, his position tense, urgent.

Upon Makil's sudden silence this one turned to look at Thora, a frown fast forming on his broad face. But he got to his feet, asking in impatient voice:

"How may we serve you, Lady?"

She eyed him for a moment before she answered. This was one who held authority. She had seen men with this air among the traders—or even among her own people when the Hunter ruled. Plainly he was just such as she sought.

"I am not the Lady," she returned coldly, "but one of Her Chosen. As to how you may serve me—let me go on my way. This is no land for me."

He looked surprised, more surprised than Makil who also watched her intently. The elder man's hand moved in a swift sign Thora knew—or it resembled one she knew. In turn she gave the recognition, one which a Chosen would use to an equal. Full belief or not, these people still held to some remnants of the Faith and thus must be recognized as distant kin.

Now the stranger spoke. What he said was garbled to Thora, the wrong inflection here and there on one of the sacred names—still it was understandable enough that she could make the required answer of ceremony.

"*She* is the beauty of the green earth, the white moon among the stars.

"To *Her* hand lies the mysteries of the waters, of the earth's growth, of the wind which caresses, of that which drives the storm.

"From *Her* all things proceed, to *Her* keeping all things return.

"Let there be beauty and strength, power and compassion, honor and humility, mirth and reverence, where *She* walks!"

Thora narrowed her small power, honed it to sharpness, stared into the open air between them, then hurled all the force she could summon. For she must show this one who and what she truly was.

There was a trembling in the air, as if something invisible fluttered there. Then there formed, for only a short instant, the sign which she wore on her inner girdle. It flickered into life and was gone again at the wink of an eye, leaving her weak and trembling with expended effort.

The valley chief gave a sharp-drawn breath. Malkin stirred, uttered one of her hissing cries, her red eyes opened, to shine coal bright.

"It would seem," Makil broke the silence first, "that there *are* others, who do walk the same Way. Do you accept this now, Borkin?"

The man was still staring at the place where the sign had appeared and vanished. Now he nodded slowly.

"One must accept the evidence of one's eyes. Who are you who can summon that?"

"I serve *Her*, being born into that service—though I am not a full initiate. There was an end to my people before I could become a vessel of full power. But *She* has fa-

vored me since so that I can call upon what
little I know and it does not fail me." Let him
at once understand that she had limits, Thora
decided. She must make no claims, which in
days to come might be proven false.

Again Borkin spoke, some words clearly,
some so twisted she did not know them for
sure. Only what he voiced were sacred things.
Though to say such thus openly—before
Makil—she wondered at this desecration of
what was to her private matters, only to be
spoken of in the shrine, and there at the proper
time. When he had finished she replied firmly:

"I know nothing of your customs. If you are
the Hunter for your people then it is true you
should know this. But it is not fitting that you
speak openly—out of proper place and time."

Borkin looked startled. "This is," he swung
back to Makil, "the ancient learning! These
people have followed the pattern as it once
was!"

Malkin slid down from Makil's lap and came
pattering across to Thora, reaching up to
catch the girl's hand which she held close to
her own down-covered cheek.

"Do you doubt now?" Makil asked. "The
sister-blood can tell—"

"But it is against—"

Thora carried the battle into his own territory. "Is it against your custom that a woman
should know such things? Well, to me, it is
against propriety that any man should say cer-

tain of the words you have just uttered.
Hunter you may be, but in our Shrine even the
Horn-Crowned does not summon without due
ritual, deferring always to the Three-In-One."

Borkin gave an impatient wave of the hand.
"It is enough for now that we do understand
the same power. That you have it at your call is
good. For this is a time when every road which
leads to the Light must converge and our
strengths added to strength, lest we be found
wanting when the Dark rises—and rising it is!
Do not mistake that!"

"You have already seen some of their handiwork," Makil's tone might not be so vehement
but it was none the less insistent. "You found
the body of Samkin—"

Malkin gave a small cry which might be one
of mourning. While Borkin took an impatient
stride down the room, then back again.

"Samkin, yes—but what of Karn?"

Makil shifted in his cushioned chair. "He is
not dead. That we would have known—"

"Where he is perhaps death would be better! We can trace his life force—yes, that still
burns. But where have they hidden him? What
use will they make of him? That we cannot
tell—"

"Unless," Makil leaned forward, his eyes on
Thora, capturing her gaze and holding it as if
he summoned will to bend her to some service

"Unless," he said again after a pause which
seemed to stretch uncomfortably long, "you

power, Chosen, being different in some ways from ours, can provide some answer—"

"What would you have me do?" She had no mind to be drawn into any affair of theirs.

"Our comrade Karn, with Samkin, his blood-brother, was sent on a scouting mission. In some way they were both entrapped. You found Samkin, my blood-sister has told me that. We have Karn's candle burning in the sanctuary. It has not gone out, thus he still lives. But in the direction he went there is now a wall of the Dark. Therefore we know he is held by the sons of Set. They can learn from him what we seek—"

Borkin took up the argument now. "And perhaps *that* is what you have already discovered, Chosen—that storage place of the past. Those of Set sought it once. But their leader died in the seeking. Malkin has told of the body you found; therefore we may surmise that either he and his people came upon that place by accident—or all those knowing of it died with him. That such places exist are old tales. The Elder Ones made safe holds against the coming of Days of Wrath. Two we have already located. But one was partly destroyed and what it contained was beyond claiming. We must have more—enough so we can bring against the Dark great force. For our numbers are few and we cannot stand against their hordes hand to hand, weapon to weapon.

"This hidden place which Malkin believes

you and she can find again—perhaps that which lies within cannot be mastered by us. But in any event it must not be left to the enemy. Just as Karn, living, must not remain in their hands. For they have ways of binding the spirit, and it may be, having wrung him dry, they could fill that emptiness with an evil brew of their own devising and send him against us—his kin! They *have* done such things—"

9

Thora stood very still. It was as if a wind from those snows still salting the peaks above had curled about her. What he had said was part of ancient and terrible legend—a story at the Craigs. Whether such a monstrous crime could indeed be, Thora did not know—but that Borkin believed it fully made an impression she was unable to push aside.

Only neither was she ready to be drawn so easily into the affairs of the valley people. That one of their blood had been taken, yes, that was a dreadful thing. But it was *they* who were kin-bound to the missing. She had taken no vengeance on those who had plundered the Craigs—for that was not the Lady's way. SHE punished in her own time. To use power as a weapon—no! No wonder these two had traveled so far from the true beliefs!

They must have read a part of her thought in her expression for Borkin's scowl grew darker while Makil—with him it was as if the natural warmth of the man had withdrawn. She had a fleeting memory of him as she had seen him in her vision—the master of the sword's flame. That was not this man.

"I cannot use any talent I have," she said slowly, "to summon power, save as the Lady works through me—and never to my own use. I do not think that you truly know HER as She is—."

"So—what will you do now?" Makil asked, his voice remote, coming to her across some chasm.

"Go forth from this valley and be about my own concerns."

Borkin smiled, no pleasant smile. "That we cannot let you do."

She was so startled by that for a moment she simply eyed him unbelievingly. A Chosen could not be so ordered—certainly not by a man!

"What then would you do to keep me—bind me with cords?"

"If the need be—yes."

Her hand fell to knife hilt. She could not accept that he would dare any such thing.

"Do you not understand?" Makil asked. "We have good reason to believe that we are under the eyes of the Dark. If you go forth from here on your lone now you would be easy meat for those who serve the Shadow. Karn was guarded, not only by a warrior's skills, but by armor of spirit—still he was taken. You have already crossed the land they claim. Who can tell what you have roused there? Traces of Power passing can be read by those trained in such trailing. They would come seeking you—"

Her hand dropped from the knife hilt to seek the gem beneath her clothing, pressing that into her flesh, as if to make it a part of her. It was true that one with Power, even as little as she believed hers to be, could sense it elsewhere. Just as she had found it in the forgotten oak wood. Had she left traces of her passing so—to be picked up by the Dark? Had perhaps that shameful cloak they had hung upon the dead tree served as a beacon?

There was a touch on her hand. Thora started, looked down at Malkin. Then she remembered that some of the furred one's blood had also passed her lips, making her free of that strange barrier in the wood.

"Just so," Makil said deliberately. "You say you are apart from us—yet the Blood Sister made pact with you. You are one of us after all."

Thora raised her other hand to rub it furiously across her lips, trying so to banish memory—the certainty that perhaps what he said was unfortunately true. She could not walk away as she wished—

Makil's face was very strained, deep shadows lay beneath his eyes. He slumped among the cushions bracing him in the chair as if he had come to the end of his strength. Borkin uttered an exclamation and went to him, while Malkin whirled away from Thora, leaping to capture both of the young man's hands, hold them tightly to her small breasts. He appeared to rouse, speaking wearily to Borkin:

"Let her rest within the outer Sanctuary. She must be with us in spirit or she cannot stand with us at all."

Borkin glanced over his shoulder to the girl. There was very little softness in that look— rather it measured her, put her on the defensive. Then he said only one word:

"Come!"

Sara appeared in the doorway to the inner rooms, hurried to Makil even as Borkin pushed open the outer portal, sweeping Thora with him. She found she could not protest as she went, Kort close beside her.

Through the edge of the village they passed, then turned into a path which was marked at intervals with standing stones. These were studded with crystals which gave a faint light like that of distant stars.

Borkin strode so swiftly that Thora's strength was further taxed. Still pride would not allow her to lag in such company. The road of the stones curved upward through the fields, still it did not draw too far from the lake—and now those stones were set closer and closer together.

She was aware that they were treading into what must be the heart of a great spiral. Farther and faster Borkin went and she followed with Kort. About this place hung a heavy silence. The night birds, the insects, of which she had been aware when they left the village, were now silent, or else all kept their distance.

Her jewel was warming. Power—yes, here was power—as yet unawakened, slumbering —but still to be sensed. And she was attuned, in spite of her denials concerning these men. There was a kinship between what she carried and a greater force abiding here.

They reached the heart of the spiral, entered from between what was now solid stone walls into an open space. This was circular and the stones guarding it gave off an even greater light. Borkin beckoned the girl forward. Reaching forth his hand he brushed fingertips across the front of her jerkin at heart level. She did not, could not, deny that he was truly an adept of the Mysteries, certainly with more power than the Hunter. Though she told herself fiercely—not the equal of the Three-In-One after they had called down the power. He sing-songed words of ritual, and to those she made her own answers.

He was, she sensed, striving to introduce

her to some force outside her own time and space—to powers which she had never dared call upon, nor would she know how. For such was granted to the Chosen only when the Lady ordained. Thora fought receiving at the hands of this stranger what she held to be the rights of her own kind.

Yet from that slight touch of his there came an inflowing of energy—which, resent it though she might, Thora could build no defense against. Borkin pointed to the pavement which was now glowing silver-white and from which a haze was rising, as might the traces of smoke from a fire of well-dried wood.

"You may try—" she removed her hand from her hidden gem. "but my power—the Lady—" She paused. No, she would offer this man no argument. Why should she? Let him see that she could not be bent in any fashion—that within herself she held defenses against what he strove to bring to life.

He did not answer, only turned from her as if his part in this act was completed. Thora watched him go. Then, because she was so tired that she could no longer pretend strength where it was not, she sank to her knees, settling cross-legged. While Kort paced slowly about the circle, his head up. Though there was something of uneasiness in his movements, he gave no direct warning, only his tail swung steadily from side to side, his lips drew back to show fangs, his eyes gleamed.

The haze about her was deepening, growing thicker. There was a pulsing surge in its rising—ebbing, flowing. She discovered that she was breathing in time to that, deep breaths which carried air into every crevice of her lungs.

Now the moon gem was so warm that it was too hot against her skin. She brought it forth, held it cupped in her hand, looking down into the surface. There also the radiance flowed. The jewel itself appeared to grow larger and larger. She was no longer aware of holding it in her hand—rather it was a vast bowl of light.

Thora sought to speak the rituals she knew, to divorce and defend herself against the ensorcellment happening. She MUST stand apart—not be encompassed by the power here. If it were meant to fill the one who sought this shrine she was not prepared to give it room. Rash assumption of power could blast the reckless. Still she was caught, and from this trap there was now no escape.

Under her feet stretched a narrow trace of way. In the dark gloom of this place it shone with the silver bright of the Lady's touch. On either hand walls stood tall, dead black as a clouded night when not even a star gleamed. From those walls came a steady beat which was like the regular pulsing of a giant heart. The earth where she now walked might itself be a living creature, lying in wait—for what

Thora could not tell.

The girl looked up, setting her head far back to catch a gleam of sky with star, if there was such here. But all she could tell was that the walls did end—well above. A wind blew about her, and that was like a puffing of breath—though it was both sharp and chill.

On she went because there was laid upon her a command she could not disobey and her faint fear subsided. Rather she sped her steps with a growing excitement, knowing a need to reach whatever nameless goal called her.

Still the path ran straight and she walked it, the walls tall beside her. There was no change in this half-alive world into which she had been wafted—or summoned. Only there was a need which she must assuage, though the manner of that service was still hidden from her.

Her feet hardly seemed to touch the ground, it might be that her will alone, or that which had sent her, bore her forward—the walls skimming past. Thus, at length, she came abruptly forth from that silt. In her now the beat of the great heart was so attuned to her own that it strengthened her. There was no fatigue of body, no stiff ache in her limbs. She was tireless.

The country into which Thora advanced was sharply etched in a strange fashion, degrees of dark, some more, some less, marked its features. Some splotches tossed branches as she was borne by them. The silver trace on the ground had vanished abruptly upon her coming into the open. Yet there was still a trail—

Thora shaped an impulse born of her will, centering on the land ahead—questing—drawing upon all she could summon. Now there sprang up on the black of the earth faint traces of silver, these shaped like the prints of naked feet. She hovered over them, unaware any more of her own body, coasting above the surface of the ground where they were set. Each was apart from the next as if they measured the stride of a man walking steadily, with a purpose. Following them she spun on into heavy darkness.

The girl was no longer aware of the heartbeat, but her excitement grew as she longed for clearer sight, a better knowledge of the land she traveled. On ran the footprints. He who had left them might have been sent to march across the world unendingly.

Thora wanted to be done with trailing—to come face to face with what lurked in this dark world. She hurled herself on, whipped by that desire.

Since the ceasing of the heavy beat, this had become a silent world. But now she became aware of another sound. Those wind-tossed branches did not sigh nor rustle, there were no calls of any bird or insect. Only, from afar, came a thump which was not that of the heart she had sensed as one with her. No, this was a drum beating with a sharp tap which stirred through the velvet darkness until she could believe its harshness made evil patterns in the air. And that troubling awoke once more her fear so she could no longer skim along, trusting the country. Rather she peered at every clump of the black, waiting for something to rise from ambush.

The dark land was coming alive, bringing alarm and the stench of peril. Now the wind carried the rotten sweetness of decay. There was death—or something worse than death ahead. Thora could not retreat, for it was toward that center of evil the footsteps she must follow marched so resolutely.

Rising from the black plain was an even denser mass—if there could be gradations of black. In this place the girl discovered that the very negation of light did possess subtle changes. The mass ahead was too regular in shape to be a hillock—nor was it a forest—

From within it came that clamor of drum or drums. The sounds they gave forth became one deep voice crying aloud, a second higher in tone, answering, with now and then a sharp rattling.

Into that mass the tracks disappeared. And into it, Thora, unable to control her going, flew after. There was an utter and complete lack of all sight for a long moment. She was stifled, buried, gasping—as if she had been flung, helpless, into a pit in the earth with sour soil heaped above. Her heart fluttered, pushed with effort, to keep life in her.

She burst out of that dark into a blaze of light which seemed blinding. At the same time the stench of old evil choked her, and a pain she could not understand made her writhe. Her answering scream was suppressed, she lacked the power to loose sound from her throat. Thus she hung in torment until she sensed that this was an assault, not upon her body (if she still had one), but rather on the core of life within it.

There came into her mind, raggedly and at first without her conscious will at all, the things she had learned. Her defenses stiffened, so slowly that she might be building a wall, stone by patiently laid stone. Still she fought and at last surrounded herself with a sphere of hard-held power. It was not enough merely to weave that for her protection—she must reach out beyond that—So had she been sent here to do.

Thus, as if she did have eyes which had to adjust to the glare after the long dark journey, she looked about her. She might be swimming in a sea of blood, for about her was a scarlet haze as thick as a fog. There were no prints to guide her. Only that faint pull. Very warily she allowed herself to be drawn along. She sent forth a probe—

Whatever she must do here must be quickly accomplished, for the threat grew ever stronger, pressing in upon her hard-held armor. To seek at the same time weakened her even more.

She followed the probe. The mist thickened and the chatter of the drums was savage—a pain through her whole person. Down in the heart of that mist shown a spark—the sign of another life force. That—that was the goal towards which she had been drawn. She gathered her strength, flashed towards it.

It was as if she looked from a high window into a cavernous room. The outer limits of its walls were so far removed they were totally hidden. But directly before her was a sharp-etched scene, vivid and alive.

Thora had found the drums and there were indeed two of them. One towered so high that he who played it must stand and lift his hands well above waist level to bring the polished bones which were his sticks down upon its painted surface. The second drummer squatted on his heels, because his instrument was a wide bowl, and the ragged edges of the skin drawn tightly across it were ringed with gleaming teeth.

Both drummers were entirely naked, their skin bleached as white as if they were growing things which had fought for life in a place where no sun ever shone. The hair on their painfully lean bodies was straggly and also near-white, caked with filth, which also smeared and stained their skins. Their eyes were turned a little upward and had no pupils, but were yellowish balls—they must be blind. While their heads and bodies swayed as they kept at the broken rhythm which made their drums seem to talk to one another—or to something which was not of human kind.

Before the drums lay a prisoner. There Thora saw the flash of light which had guided her. She dropped her probe, realizing that such could reveal her presence to her own peril. Stretched on the pavement lay a man also bare of body. His chest arched with every breath, as if he fought for air, while around him were filaments of black cords which had their birth in the drums—curling up, weaving about his flesh. These grew ever darker and thicker, though sometimes they slipped when on that laboring breast the flare would brighten—fighting their power.

This captive was not pale of skin like the drummers. Sun had touched him to a deeper brown, and his hair was a shining cap. Thora knew him for one of the valley men.

Yes, he was still fighting with all the strength he could summon, against what they would do with him. As if a finger touched Thora's mind, opening thus a door she had not known existed, she understood what they would do and what he fought against. The talking drums—if they wove well their spell —would encase him wholly, even as certain insects wove coccoons about their own bodies—then issue forth in time quite changed in form for the rest of their lives. So he would come out of the drum weaving different —different and utterly vile!

The drummers were tireless, the prisoner had been drawn nearly to the end of his supply of strength, using to the full every defense he knew. There would come a time very soon when the last flicker of that power would die and he would lie full within the net—to become a thing which could be turned against those of his own blood.

Thora had been summoned to this battle— but not as a spectator. About her the field of protective force she held so desperately quivered. How long she might keep that intact the girl dared not even guess. What was demanded of her? She strove to free herself of the compulsion which held her. This was no war of hers—

Only, even as that denial crossed her consciousness, she knew shame. Different powers might they own, this helpless man and she, but there was a single goal—when evil roved abroad both of them held to the path of Light.

Slowly, because she was so aware of the danger of what she did, Thora fumbled to fashion a weapon which was the only one she could use here. She held to the force of her mind the image of her throwing spear—its point blazing with silver fire—that of the Lady—cold flame—the more deadly.

There was no throwing stick to hurl it, she

could put no force of arm in what she would do—only her own will and determination. Thora poised her thought—hurled it with all her strength, though her web of protection withered and was like a tattered cloak, no good against what gathered here.

She forced herself to think of nothing but the spear—the silver point. Down she sent that, straight at the taut skin of the taller drum. She could not see any weapon, she could only believe it existed. There was a flash of light before the blind drummer. The tight skin burst, became shriveled rags. He was thrown back as the drum overturned, rolling to one side, to strike full upon the shoulder of the seated drummer, knocking him in turn face down upon his own instrument.

The spear was gone—Thora could not summon that again. Yes—there was the knife! That knife which had been so long in the possession of believers that it must have gathered to it greater power. Thora readied her picture of that, forced what remained of her energy into it, sent its point at the smaller drum where the player struggled to hold the bowl straight. Again came a flash—a breaking.

Thora was whirled about, driven as a leaf, powerless to combat the second surge of released power—unseeable but deadly. She fought to pull about her the remnants of her earlier protection. Only she was swept along by the force, borne away from the drummers, not knowing whether her aid had helped the prisoner or not.

Deaf, blind, helpless-borne—even her thoughts churned and broken— The dark held her—it was seeping into her—cutting her off from the living world. She held onto life by the smallest thread, felt herself twisted this way and that, as if a greater force strove so to break that frail hold. She would not be bested! Not yet—not here! She would hold!

Power, a crushing force lashed out, wrapped around her, drew her from the maelstrom which had caught her. Once more she was in motion. Yet she also knew that what drew her was not the same force which had guided her to the drummers, though it was darkly malific.

Sight returned. She flew along between high pointed arches. Beneath her on square pillars torches burned with an oily smoke from where they were thrust into rings of rusty metal. These gave but limited light. Nothing moved here. Only for a moment did she see that chamber or hall. Then what held her gave a sharp upward jerk.

Thora arose—passing through stone as if that were but illusion. Illusion? Illusions were known to all. There were ways to break the hold of such. Her thought fastened desperately on that hope. This was an illusion—it had to be!

But were *they* also illusions—the three whom the compelling force brought her to confront? In a circle of dark they stood plainly forth because their cloaks gave a shimmering burst of color—red cloaks on which crawled and spun, as they flung their arms wide to show the inner, symboled lining, the vilest of signs. They knew she was there—they had found her.

Somehow that very belief steadied Thora. These Dark ones had expected something —someone—else she sensed. They were not prepared for her. Therefore, perhaps just perhaps—she had some small advantage.

The two outer of the trio wore their hoods well pulled down over their heads so she could see little of their faces, only a slice of chin—with skin as pallid as that of the drummers. As the drummers they were also nude of body, but across their skins were marks which enforced those symbols on their cloaks—on the breast above the heart—encircling their loins. And those marks glistened—blood might be oozing out to keep them brilliant.

He who stood between the two was not masked, the hood of his cloak was folded back upon his shoulders. His face was that of a young man, save that across the skin wove a thousand small wrinkles. The youth might be a mask, cracking with time's passing to show the age beneath. His hair was pale yellow and he wore it short, though not cropped into a cap as did the valley men. Rather it grew in tight, sculptured curls.

His eyes were dark—so dark and sunk beneath the arch of his brows that they might not be there at all—only pits in his face. Between them his nose was a sharply defined beak, save that it possessed thick nostrils turned upward. While his mouth stretched too wide to be wholly that of any man—thick lipped—showing the points of two fangs on the drooping lower stretch of red.

It was the face of a monster—it was also the face of one who had for long, very long, commanded power. That power appeared now to stream forth, creating a cloud about him. He turned his head a fraction from one side to the other, and there was something in the gesture which made Thora guess that, while he sensed her presence here, he could not see her as she saw him.

10

Though his two companions kept their arms outstretched, baring the symbols on the interior of their cloaks and those painted on their own bodies, the hoodless man now tossed the edges of his single garment over his shoulders, brought his hands into the air to begin, with swift, sure strokes, drawing the invisible upon the invisible. Only what he produced was becoming visible in thin, scarlet lines—

Thora experienced a tightening about her body. (But did she possess a body here?) At least there was some container for her spirit which acted in that fashion and was now growing heavier, dragging her, she believed, into a form with which this Dark One could easier deal.

Against the Dark stood the Light. She could not easily call upon the Lady in the very heart of enemy domain (of that she was also certain), or use the same tactics which had defeated the drums. No—she must fasten on something greater—more powerful than any vision of spear or knife. Fasten upon that which only the Lady might lay hand on—

The girl strove to shut out sight of the Dark One, thrust aside the fear that he was about to entomb her in a form he could deal with. A disc of silver white—the Moon at its full when it hung above a sacred grove at that time when the Mother's powers waxed the strongest, could that be summoned—to fight?

One of the priest's white hands twisted sharply at the wrist, bent back in a way which certainly he had not willed. Across his knuckles flashed a white spark, even such as had flickered on the breast of the prisoner before the drums.

The man's thick lips pulled back in such a snarl as Kort's. His other hand slapped at that spark as if he strove to banish an insect.

Moon—the full moon!

Thora did not have her gem to pull its rays, to hold its power. Yet she had indeed counterattacked this Dark Lord. In the very heart of his own citadel (for Thora was sure that was where she now was) the force of his Enemy had struck—if only for an instant.

Thus heartened Thora threw at him a vision

of the Lady's Lamp—the full orb of silver.

His snarl held just as *she* held with desperation to that mind vision. Surprise had won the girl an earlier fraction of easement. Now he would bring to bear the full force of his power. Against that Thora would be but a leaf in a storm. She could only, as that other captive had done, fight as long as there was any energy left in her.

Hopelessly, she faced the Dark One, tried to build to aim—to summon—only to have it slip away—

Until—

Thora flinched as if a knife had entered her body, aimed by a foeman she had not known was there. Save she realized in a second that this new force had not come to harm, to drain. Instead there fed into her such a welling spring of power that she did not know if she could contain or master it. Mentally she envisioned herself now standing in a sacred grove, her hands up and out, her fingers pointing at the Dark Lord heart-high. She could not see such hands in truth, she dared not even break the gaze of her eyes upon his face for fear she might weaken that which was feeding through her.

Sparks danced in the air, to become larger, fuller. These were those same creatures of light she had run along the beam cast by the sword in her earlier vision. They hurled themselves at the Dark Lord.

Even if he might be blind to the nature of the attack, he felt the force of it. He staggered, half-fell against the body of his companion on the right, so that that man, plainly astounded, had to steady his master.

Out of Thora continued to leap those things born of light. There were fewer of them now, she could feel the ebb of strength which fed them. The Dark Lord straightened, threw off the support of his follower.

Only his short loss of control brought about Thora's release. She was out of that chamber as if awakening from a dread dream. Here was thick dark again. Still, in this crawled no evil. Once more began the beating of that great heart which moved the world, and she rested, feeling its comfort, slipping away from what had been great danger into—

She opened her eyes wide. Here was no dark. Tall gleaming stones stood sentinel. Kort pushed against her whining. His tongue swept across her cheek. Above was not the clouded night sky but the grayness of dawn. However what she saw was not Kort's anxious eyes, not the stones, nor anything else but the hilt of a sword held over her—the single great gem in it flaming high. From that radiated warmth, life, a strong barrier against all evil.

"You had no right to send her so!"

Did she hear those words with the ears of her body, or had they flowed into her mind, meaning without sound?

"She was not sent. There was that in her which awoke to Karn's need and she answered."

"And was near taken for it!"

"She professes to be one who follows the true path—"

"Which you cannot deny!" The first voice interrupted hotly. "Therefore, having brought her to a source of the Force, you left her in its influence. What would have chanced at the end, do you think, had she not been drawn forth by the Weapon of Lur? Are those with power to be used as tools, to have no purpose nor meaning otherwise? Have we not fought the Dark for that very reason—among others—that no will is to be enslaved, as is true where the Shadow spreads? If we use the methods of the Enemy are we any better then than they?"

Yes, these were spoken words and not just thoughts in her mind. The glory of the sword's gem was dimming as if the fire within it died. So Thora could see beyond to him who held it protectingly over her.

How could it be Makil? When she viewed him last he had seemed an invalid, unable to leave his chair without help. Yet here he stood as vigorous as any armsman she had seen march in protection with a trader's convoy— such a man as prided himself on strength of arm, the readiness of his body to give and receive blows.

To one side, still facing him, was Borkin, a frown on his face, a twist to his lips, as if he did not readily accept any rebuke. In him she felt a coldness which was not to be easily melted by the inner fire of the younger man.

The sword swung up and back, and Makil allowed the blade to slip through his fingers until his flesh covered the fading color of the gem. With practiced ease he slid the weapon then into a sheath he wore behind his shoulder. Once that was done he stooped, his fingers closed about the girl's right wrist, held firmly, as if he would make sure that the life-blood still pulsed steadily through her veins.

"I am here," Thora gathered voice. She tried to throw off his hold, but he would not loose it. "I think," purposefully she ignored Borkin, spoke directly to the younger man. "that I have now much to owe you."

That it was Makil, and what power he could summon, which had drawn her away from that confrontation with the three Dark Ones she had no doubt. What strength he had! With such men as these why did the valley have any fear that the Dark would prevail.

He loosed her wrist. She had a feeling that during those few moments he had been made as uncomfortable by that contact as she. Now he moved a little back and set his shoulders against one of the stones guarding this place as though he needed such support.

A smaller figure came running down the spiral opening to this shrine, flung itself at Makil, catching at one of his dangling hands and planting that firmly upon its own shoulder. Malkin was here, and it was plain she was alarmed concerning her blood-brother.

Thora felt drained, emptied as she never had before. But her stubborn pride made her sit up, lock her hands one upon the other, hold her head high, and she hoped, unwaveringly.

"I do not know where I traveled—" now she spoke to Borkin, "but there I saw your Karn. They tried to weave about him some netting born of their drums. Later there were three others in red cloaks—and one of those—" she strove to keep her voice level, to conquer any sign of fear, "is a man of very great power."

"Some such as doubtless counts a number of skulls in his walls," Borkin returned.

His meaning was strange, until Thora recalled an old tale—that those of the Dark were reputed to so set the remains of the enemies, believing that they so imprisoned, even controlled in part, the essence of those who had fallen to their attack.

"Such a one," she agreed. The girl was glad that she had so far not betrayed to either of these two her great weariness, and—worse —her fear. She had not lost that, even when drawn away from the dark source. At that moment Thora was not sure whether she could rise and walk. Her limbs seemed as weak as if she had lain days in a bed of fever. She longed for a rest or a full cup of herb-brewed honey mead such as was given always to those who served the Lady by vision calling.

Kort nudged against her, offering the comfort he sensed she needed, which neither of these valley men might give. She threw an arm about the hound's wide shoulders and again his tongue wiped lovingly across her cheek.

"Do you know where lies this place of the Dark Ones?" she asked. "I left your Karn free of the binding they would set on him. However they may have other spellings, and he still lies within their hands."

Borkin nodded. "That is so. Still he lives, and you found him. What is seen by the eye of the spirit can be followed by the eye of the body. We now have a guide to Karn—"

She was startled into speechlessness. Having used her once out of body, did they now expect to employ her again? March her across country into the very heart of the Dark to free a man who meant nothing to her? Expect her to once more front a Dark One of great power? Truly this Borkin *did* consider her a tool! But she was not, as he would speedily discover.

Deep in his throat Kort growled. He swung about his heavy head so his yellow eyes watched the older valley man. Perhaps from the tensing of Thora's muscles where her arm rested upon him he had read her anger. That the hound was not to be mastered easily either was now plain.

A chittering cry from Malkin cut through the mounting tension. Both girl and man looked to where Makil had stood. He had slid down the pillar supporting him, only his head and upper shoulders still resting against the stone. With an exclamation Borkin pushed past Thora to kneel beside the young man.

Just for a moment did the girl hesitate. Then she arose stiffly and with her hand upon Kort's head, her hide boots making no sound, she wavered to the opening of the spiral, passing on through the light of early morning, to turn her back upon those of the valley and their concerns.

As she went Thora argued within herself. Certainly she owed Makil for her escape, but just as certainly she was sure his own people, in the person of Borkin, had somehow arranged that night journey using her. Therefore, having freed Karn—if she had—the scales were balanced. She owed them nothing, and Makil had his own kind to nurse him. She would find her way out of this valley, forget it existed. There was too much here which threatened her in ways she did not understand and could not defend herself against. This was no clear-cut battle of the Light against the Dark—rather it was a struggle between two ways of life. And to withdraw from such was no act of cowardice, instead one of prudence for a Chosen.

Free of the shrine Thora adapted for her

journey across the valley the same tactics she would have used in any strange countryside, letting Kort scout, being as sure as she could that she herself passed unseen.

She was tired, also she knew she must have time to think of a way past the defenses in the heights. If Borkin planned to make further use of her as an unwilling guide to that place of the Dark, then those outer guards would be alerted not to let her pass. She could hope for a little time, while Borkin was concerned with Makil. However, that time might be short—

At the thought of the sword Makil bore she shook her head. That was a mighty talisman or focus of Power—such as she had heard of in legends. As such it could not be a threat to her.

The Three-In-One had their ritual knives, their wands, their cups—yes. But though these might hold power for a short space—no one could deliver such a lance of force as she had seen twice now issue from the hilt of that weapon. Her own gem was nothing compared to that. The valley men had learned mighty secrets—Very well: let them now employ them against the Dark.

Against the Dark—According to them the Dark was rising, lapping farther and farther out from whatever foul source fed and maintained it. She had felt the power of those drums. As for the cloaked Three—especially he who commanded them—even the Old Ones of the Three-In-One after long years of their

Calling Down—might not be reckoned his
equal. It was treason to all Thora believed to
admit that, but she must reluctantly face the
truth.

Still these valley men could also have other
strong resources beside the sword. Only, if
they possessed such, why had *she* been used to
hunt out Karn? The girl shook her head deter-
minedly as she slipped along a hedge dividing
two fields, following where Kort led. Soon the
sun would be up, then she would be a fool to
seek a way out by day. She must find shelter in
which to rest and break her fast from the
scanty supplies remaining in her pack. Now
she motioned to Kort, saw him move on, hunting a hiding place.

They found hiding in a small wood where
there was brush enough to form a screen. Kort
crept on his belly into the heart of that growth,
and Thora, going flat and pushing her pack before her, wriggled after, into a hollow which
she enlarged with her knife to fit them better,
packing the lengths she had cut to curtain the
passage they had used.

The ground was damp and there were flies
which bit viciously until the girl brought out a
box of greasy herb mixture and used it, rubbing the stuff over her face and arms, and
drawing fingers of it down Kort's hide. Then,
with her head pillowed on the hound's side,
knowing that he was better than any human
watchman, Thora allowed herself to sleep.

The sleep was not deep. Rather she dozed and woke, then dozed again. Grimly she practiced the disciplines she had been taught to relax mind and body. But her last night's venture had left her as distraught as she had not been since her first vigil under the Lady's great lamp. It was hard to shut out of her mind the thoughts of the Dark.

Was it true that much of the world outside this well-guarded cup was now patrolled by the enemy? She knew well that any use of power within a land over which the Shadow fell would alert those who served it, that perhaps they had some who could sniff her out even as Kort nosed out the trail of a wild cow. However, it was better to chance such a peril on her own than remain tamely on hand for Borkin and his kind to use as they willed.

First she must get out of the valley, win back into the outer world where she had roamed without more than normal caution. Perhaps it would be well to head east once more. There must have been other survivors of the Craigs. Perhaps even the Three-In-One had found refuge in the broken lands a little to the north. Why had she roamed so from there? Looking back now Thora realized that she had broken a long-held pattern of her people by scouting west and she could not understand why.

She brought her jewel from beneath her clothing. Folding her hands palm to palm with its cool stone tightly clasped between, she fought to empty her mind, to pass into the Way wherein the Lady, should SHE have reason, might give her counsel—for that she needed above all else.

No vision answered her endeavors—only sleep at last, which was deep and restful and from which she awoke as Kort nuzzled her ear, coming instantly alert, feeling as one who has fed, drank and slept well. This new strength must be the answer from the Lady—her body and mind prepared so for what lay ahead.

They ate again of her supplies. Within the valley she would not dare to hunt, nor must Kort, close to any homestead. And it might be long until she could win past the heights. It was already past sundown, and the walls of the valley shut off those rays early. Dusk was drawing in as Thora wriggled back through the brush to peer out.

There were buildings within sight, several fields away from the wood. She watched a lamp blaze up in a window there. Kort sniffed, testing the wind. In the failing light his tail moved once, an old signal. There was no one near.

Still the hound kept to the edge of the wood, and then along some hedging which separated one field from another. There were sheep grazing which stirred uneasily as the two passed. Thora wondered just how many people there were in the valley. Martan had spoken of those who, unable to find family ties, went out into the world. Karn must have been such a roamer.

Then there were the sentries in the wall forts. But Thora's stay there had been so limited she could not guess whether there were those who traveled much across the cup itself. She believed that they must round the end of the lake if she were to win back to the same stairway down which they had come. On the other hand, that road was so well guarded she could not hope to pass out so. She busied herself with the making and discarding of many half-plans, all of which proved to possess an outstanding flaw.

Surely there must be more than one way into the valley—even if that were guarded. She would have to leave the immediate future to the Lady. The farther she went, she could see that the valley was more of an oval than she had believed, and it ran well to the north.

Hedged fields gave way to pasturage. They crept by two more buildings showing small lights. No dogs barked, and Thora began to believe that such companions as Kort were unknown to these people.

The upper end of the valley was in a far wilder state—if wilderness meant unchecked growth of trees and brush. She discovered one small irregular field recently dug over, and stumbled across a heap of root vegetables of last year's growing. Pausing, she harvested those of the withered discards which were still edible, stopping again when they came to a stream to wash them as well as drink her fill and see her water bottle refilled. Here Kort did go hunting, to return with a rabbit, she leaving him the whole of his kill since she dared not light a cookfire.

Rested and refreshed after a scanty fashion, they went on. When the first morning light shone, they were in a wood which Thora was sure stretched to the cliff foot. Even though they had seen no pursuit, she knew very well they were far from freedom. Those of the valley might consider them safely pent within that trap and had turned their attention momentarily to other things—sure of their prey when they wanted them.

Again she slept with the moon gem between her hands. Only this time she also pillowed her head on those hands with a vague idea she could so fortify her mind against any invasion. Twice in the early dawn she had burrowed deeper under bushes when a winged windrider cruised above, uncertain whether their sight was keen enough to note her.

Her sleep was once more dreamless. Only, when she woke at Kort's alert, she did so with a feeling of uneasiness. This grew as time wore on. The wood protected them from sighting from the air—but in her was a need for haste.

NO!

It came as a blow which near sent her reeling. As in that wood outside, she once again met an invisible barrier. The valley men were using their power! Trying to hold her, perhaps even draw her back, as a hooked fish must obey the pull of the line. Only Thora was not a fish, nor was she helpless. The girl brought out her jewel, pressed it to her forehead. The sensation was as if she bathed her face in cool water. That tug lessened, and she could fight it.

How long did she battle so? In such times the world's reckoning of moments did not measure. As suddenly as it had exerted that pull the pressure was gone. However, she kept the gem clasped tight and stumbled ahead, unmindful of the briars lashing at her, determined only to put space between her and the source of that compulsion. If they could not succeed in controlling her one way, they would surely try another.

Thora stumbled twice before she learned that the ground was rising. Because of the darkness and the thick growth she could not tell if she had reached the valley rim. Kort padded steadily on. The brush began to thin, there was a mass of tumbled stone in which was stuck the splintered trunks of trees caught by some old avalanche. Kort kept to the top of a rock, pointed with his nose toward where brush had began to mask the scar, and gave a short bark.

Here indeed was a wall. Because of the

night, Thora could not see any handholds for climbing. Also the debris was dangerous footing, she dreaded a fall— Instead she waved Kort north again.

They sheltered that day on the fringe of the avalanche where a vast tumble of earth and stone spilled into the valley. Again Thora tried to sleep under the Lady's blessing—encouraged because now the sickle of a new moon would show very thin—a promise. The Maid was riding the skies tonight and SHE might well look upon a young servant with favor.

So she slept through the day, waiting for that night and the moon. This was no vision such as her journey through the Dark world had been. No, she was bathed in silver light and before her was the barrier she had followed with such reduced hope. However, Thora now could spy a dark crack like a doorway, and she knew that this was the way to freedom, and that it was her own Lady who had led her to it. She was still one with the Power she had always served—what lay before her was no trap. It was right and fitting that a Chosen go this way.

No vision—she was not asleep—she was standing so—though she did not know how she had come here. She looked up to the sickle moon, kissed her gem, and held that up to its light gratefully.

Then with it in her right hand—the other

resting on Kort's shoulder, Thora went confidently on into this way which had been shown to her.

11

The break in the cliff was not an entrance to a cave, but rather gave upon an upward climb —easy at first, but growing harder. With Thora's dislike of heights she was somewhat glad that it was night. And she was careful not to look back or down as she made a cautious search for handholds ahead. Luckily the slope was not severe, Kort took it before her, and now and then there came a rattling stone dislodged by the hound's passage.

It widened out so that the sides did not rasp against her back and she had room to move—always up. Then, though walls still hemmed about her, the track became roughly level.

The night thickened about them. Thora used

her spear to tap out the way ahead. There were no lines of silver here to guide the traveler. At last the crevice gave away and she came out on a ledge which she believed to lie on the other side of the valley walls.

Kort had given no warning. If there were sentries here—or any post at all—the hound must have decided those no danger. This ledge overhung a descent which looked too steep to be taken without a rope. But, to her horror, she saw Kort gather himself for a leap and launch straight out into the open air. That the hound had gone mad or was possessed, was her first reaction. Then she threw herself belly down, pulling inch by cautious inch to the lip of the drop to peer below.

She saw movement, heard a subdued crackling. It was plain that Kort had survived his leap, not only survived but was uninjured. For a moment later, there sounded a soft whine which was one of his signals that all was well. To follow him blindly was an act demanding such determination of will that Thora fought a battle with herself. There remained though only one alternative, an ignominious return to the valley—an admission that her courage had failed her. That she would not allow.

The girl wriggled on, allowed her body to slip sidewise while keeping a hold on the ledge, then set her teeth and let go, striving to relax as she fell. She tumbled straight into a mass of sharp-scented vegetation which, crushed under her weight, gave forth an acrid odor strong enough to set her coughing. On she rolled until Kort's teeth in her belt caught and held so she could lever herself up.

What she had seen of the upward rise of these heights upon their entrance into the valley had been mainly barren country with only a few weather-stunted trees and twisted brush. In spite of the dark she could make out here a thick tangle of vegetation, spongy, springy and odorous—though the scent, once she became used to it, was not too unpleasant.

Kort loosed his hold and nudged at her thigh with his head, urging her on. There seemed at first to be no way through this mass except that gained by simply floundering along. Then she stumbled out into what was perhaps a game trail, at least a way clear ahead.

The growth waved feathery fronds well above her head. In spite of the chill of the heights, this vegetation was thick-set rather like a moss which had grown giant enough to suggest a grove. All she brushed against during her passage brought no hard branch to impede her progress. Kort trotted on, not ranging far as was his usual wont on the trail.

As they went the fronds grew even taller, meeting overhead to shut out both slender moon and sky. But there were odd, pale flowers or rounded blossoms shaped like moon-silver cups tinged with faint blue or green. These shed a haze of phosphorescence, while about them winged insects which also flashed light from their small bodies.

From the cup flowers arose also a subtle scent, not acrid like that of the mass into which she had fallen, but instead a delicate perfume which must be what drew the flyers, so that they came to cling, weighing down the blossoms of their choice. Their gauzy wings beat the air with a constant busy hum. It was such a place she had never seen, even in a vision. Yet she knew that this was as real as her own feet treading the narrow way.

A slow change began in this wood—some of the fronds now had thicker boles, became closer in size to saplings, then to trees. The light flowers were still thick, but now they nodded from vines which wreathed those trees, forming so close a tangle that Thora believed she could not have forced a way from the narrowly open path. It seemed those growing walls were to screen secrets—for there were secrets here. She sensed a touch, fleeting, faint—within her—as if delicate fingers had reached out in curiosity to examine who had invaded this peaceful place, striving so to measure her in a fashion beyond her reckoning.

The flowers, too, grew larger—their scent stronger. Thora found it more difficult to keep her attention fixed upon the need for going on. With lagging steps she fought a desire to stretch out beside the path—close her eyes—

Startled, the girl looked down at the moon gem where it now swung outside her clothing. There was no angry clouding of a warning there. She felt power but of a new kind— Whatever it was owed no allegiance to the Dark.

Then, even as she had felt the beating of the world's heart during her journey, now she sensed a rhythm also in this place, a soft cadence which could not be heard, but which crept into one's flesh and bones—

Thora found herself drawing deep, even breaths in time to that stimulus. The fatigue which should have weighed her down faded, and she was filled with well being.

She was not sure when the singing began. It must have been a part of that which had entered into her before she separated it from the rest. Also, muted and afar as it seemed, she knew this of old, for she had heard Malkin so summon when Thora had danced for the Lady. Save this was not voiced by a single one of the furred people as it had been when she had danced before Malkin—but rather by how many—?

The path ended in a clearing where the vine-ladened trees were full sheathed in blossoms, so that there was a mist of light. Winged feasters flitted back and forth across the open, buzzing loudly, but not so as to drown out that other sound.

Here were furred ones indeed, seated cross-

legged, even as Thora had seen Malkin sit
upon the outspread cloak. Save that these
were cushioned from the ground by drifts of
fallen blossoms. Though those had been culled
from the vines they did not look withered or
bruised, only from them arose such a wave of
fragrance that Thora wavered. Her booted feet
slipped on the fringes of that carpet and she
went to her knees, Kort halting beside her.

Yet none of the singers turned to look at her.
Instead their red eyes ablaze, they faced the
center of their circle where moved a single female of their species.

Even as Thora had danced so did this slender, down-covered body weave and leap, glide
and sway. Clawed hands swung a long, thickly
plaited garland of the flowers, and, now and
then, she advanced on some member of that
seated circle, tossed a loose loop about his or
her shoulders and held it so for a breath or
two, before withdrawing once again into the
circle's heart.

Thora found that she could not rise to her
feet. Her body would not obey her will. She too
began to sway in answer to the hissing croon
raised by those who appeared so ensorcelled
by some bright vision of their own.

There stirred in Thora's memory what had
been said about the youths of the valley—that
they went to a wood where they met with the
furred ones, and those who were chosen came
forth again with familiars. Thus she believed

that she must have strayed into this place sacred to such as Malkin. Here the furred ones wove their own webs of power. She was awed—she who had faced the Dark—for there was something here of a force like unto her own—only stronger—wilder in its own way.

Suddenly in her mouth once again was that biting, acrid taste of Malkin's blood. This was no place for her, warned something, save that she could not obey any such warnings. She could only kneel and watch as the dancer spun her own enchantment, flinging out the wreath to draw one of her fellows into a momentary sharing of high ecstasy. That much Thora knew without the telling. One danced and the power filled one, then—even as she, Thora, passed her own power through the moon gem—so did this one now relay what she had gathered on to her fellows.

Thora took her jewel between her hands—to strengthen her—to ward off this alienness. The stone was chill and the cold of it fought against the cloying scent of the flowers and cleared her head.

With the release of her mind there followed compulsion of another kind. Not entirely aware of what she did, Thora got to her feet. She had dropped her pack, and now with one hand she sought the fastenings of her garments, keeping the other cupped tight about the gem. Leather and linen fell from her body. Here was no moonlight to bathe her—the

Maiden was far too slim and new-born to give
true sustenance. Yet her feet moved, her body
tensed, as along it ran the summons which before only the Lady's own light had awakened
in her.

Fatigue and bemusement were gone. She
leaped, she skimmed through the air as if she
wore the wings of the Windriders. Over the
heads of the furred ones that leap carried her.
Then she came lightly to earth beside their
dancer. The glowing red eyes of the flower-
bearer looked upon her, accepted her. Thora
began to follow the earlier pattern of the
other's in-and-out steps, circling around the
furred one who no longer tossed her garland
to one of her people but stood, feet planted to
earth, body swaying sensuously, the flower
string now wound tight about her, now tossed
out by the movements of her arms and shoulders.

In and out—always facing the furred one
who turned with her so they continued to lock
eyes. And from that locking came communication:

"Hail—moon daughter—" In Thora's mind
the words formed clearly. "Long has it been
since one touched by the Mother has sought us
out."

Not out of Thora's conscious memory came
her answer—yet it was in her mind sharply
and clear.

"Hail, you of the blood kin. Like greets like

along the Road."

The furred dancer made a graceful gesture of greeting and the end of her flower rope flashed out to touch Thora's breast just above the sign of the Chosen. It was as if a pointed finger had pressed against her with some force, bringing with it a sense of comradeship, of sharing. Not as those of the valley would share with these—that she knew now. This sharing was of a different degree—even stronger in its own way. Far from like they might be in body, even in mind—but the dancer was a spirit who had long walked the White Path and perhaps once she, too, had danced for the moon.

"Just—so—" Thora received an answer to that thought. "There is no end to true life, only changes brought about by time, and time does not indeed bind us as we think when within this one short life. Welcome, sister—"

The furred one held out a clawed hand and Thora in turn reached out with hers in which the moon gem lay. Their fingers met and clasped about the stone. From one to the other and back again flowed the force of what they summoned. So it was as if they drank together a strange but restoring wine.

Then the dancer went to her knees and Thora knelt beside her—finally discovering it better to stretch her body along the ground, propping herself up on her elbows so that she and the dancer could remain eye to eye. Dimly she was aware that these who had formed the circle were slipping quietly away, melting back into the vine tapestried walls of the wood, leaving the two of them alone.

"The Dark rises—" There was no struggle to voice words such as Malkin had had to make. The furred one might hiss but Thora could readily understand.

"The Dark is strong," she replied.

Those eyes blazed with such strength Thora seemed to feel all the heat of the emotion behind them. "Then we must be stronger. The brothers move to battle. What do you?"

Was there dissatisfaction, a rebuke in that? Thora was not sure, but she was uncomfortable. Though she felt no kinship with the valley people, though she resented what she believed that Borkin, at least, had tried to use her for—still it was true that, though they might not be comrades, the Enemy was common to them both.

"I am not one of them—" the girl began defensively. "I stand alone in this land." It did not seem strange that she could speak and the other readily understand, that the furred one might hiss in her own language and that now Thora found that intelligible. In this place of enchantment anything might well happen.

"You are one through which Another acts—" the furred one returned. "Not for such as you and I the blood bond—"

"That is so." Thora felt relief. Though the

valley men could accept such a kinship, and proudly, yes, she understood that a little. But she was not one to follow such a way. In spite of need she would shrink from that linkage, and blood bond must be between two who willed it with all their hearts.

"So—for us it is thus—" Again the claw hand linked with hers over the moon gem. "In this way we strengthen one another. I am Tarkin—"

"And I Thora." The exchange of true names, that, too, was a bond—a link which Thora well understood.

"Together then we shall go—" Tarkin nodded vigorously, her gleaming eyes still alight with their deepest fire.

"Into the dark—" Thora knew, was forced to accept that. There might be no escape. What she did now was a part of the weaving after all, she had to surrender her own will to that belief. She had not really drifted without purpose when the Craigs fell. No, all she had done since that hour of the raiders had been wrought on the loom of the Mother. So this was her fate.

"Into the Dark, sister of the moon." The furred one's hand lifted from above the jewel. Then claw tips touched her lightly, so very lightly, on her lips, before rising to trace a symbol on her forehead. "But first you shall rest, and only when the hour ordained comes will we go."

Thora carried from that moment only the dimmest of memories. She had fallen asleep on the carpet of unfading flowers, watching still Tarkin seated nearby, those blazing eyes near closed. The other had crooned softly so that a thread of sound lulled the girl into slumber.

The first rays of the sun rising in splendor crossed the sky when she awoke. Under her the flowers had withered at last, quickly fallen away into skeletons of themselves so that they remained only the tracery of long dead petals, though their perfume still clung to her skin. Tarkin was gone, nor was there anyone else within that circle of open glade save Kort, his muzzle deep in a bowl of polished wood. Beside her was another such bowl, but smaller, in which was a mixture of fine-ground, moistened grain with dried fruit, and beside that a bottle filled with green liquid.

The sight of the food brought an instant response of hunger and Thora fell upon the offering greedily. Beside her also were the garments she had discarded, neatly folded, and beyond them her pack. She ate, then dressed, looking about her. The vines on the trees appeared to be thickly interwoven, enough so that one could not force a way between and she hesitated to raise knife to slash at them. One did not take any life wantonly here—even that of a vine—she was sure of that. Was she then to go back down the path which led her here—return to the valley, having at last accepted that there was no freedom of choice for her?

As Thora hesitated a section of vine was swept back, as one might gather up the folds of a door curtain, and Tarkin stood there. Though all furred people looked so alike, the girl was sure that this was the dancer. They had shared that which would always make them known to one another.

"It is time—"

Again Thora understood the hissing without any great effort to communicate as Malkin had had to make. "The Dark does not wait—even as night itself does not follow the pleasure of man—"

Stooping to pass beneath the droop of that vine curtain the girl found herself entering another path, one which ran as straight as that which had brought her to the clearing. Tarkin padded ahead, Kort pushed close between them, and the girl trotted to keep up.

Those flowers which had furnished light and scent had closed into green or blue-white balls and there were no insects gathered about them. Nor were there any other signs of life within the wood. If the furred ones watched their going, none allowed him or herself to be seen. The three moved alone, shut out now from the life which filled this place.

Once more they issued from wood into the tall, moss-bedded ferns, and then from them into knee high growth, able to see ahead a long slope into the plains lands. Overhead swooped one of the winged sentinels. Thora had no reason today to conceal herself. With Tarkin she felt that she was about a lawful business which those of the valley must recognize. If the Windrider wanted to report her passing to his leaders—then let him do so.

At midday they paused and ate. Thora discovered that not only had her water flask been refilled, but also the lean food pouches within her pack were again plump with the meal and fruit mixture which she ate in handfuls, giving Kort the last of her dried meat for he seemed in no readiness to go hunting but stayed close at hand.

On they trailed, well out of the fringe growth of the wood of the furred ones into first the arid rock, and then scantily grown over earth of the heights, finally into meadowland. Tarkin went as a guide here, confidently as if she followed a well marked road. Even Kort yielded place to her. They were striking due west. From time to time Thora surveyed the land ahead narrowly—it teased her mind that perhaps she could recognize here some small clue to that country she had transversed in her night vision.

Kort hunted for his supper, bringing Tarkin a fresh kill as he always had Malkin. But the furred one gently refused that—saying that only those who were paired (as she expressed it) must be supplied with blood—for when they took the bond of kinship their bodies were in a manner changed. Since she had made no such tie with Thora, she would remain an eater of grain and fruit, and she carried her own pouch of supplies.

They spent the night in a thicket much the same as the one Kort had discovered in the valley, and in the morning, just after dawn, came to a stream where there was a pool deep enough for Thora to splash in waist-high and for her companion to duck under. They washed, the girl drying her body with handfuls of last year's grass pulled from about the roots of the new crop, Tarkin applying her long tongue to her pelt as a cat might lick dry and groom.

Thus refreshed, they followed the stream, even though it curved somewhat to the north. They had not gone far before Kort suddenly faced their backtrail, growling. Thora dodged behind the nearest boulder which afforded a partial defense. Tarkin did not follow her.

Instead the furred one uttered a hissing call, her head well back on her shoulders as if to release that to the farthest reach. And she was answered.

Out of the willows bordering the stream on the other side came a male of Tarkin's people and behind him—Malkin! Nor were the two alone for here also came Martan, shorn of wings, walking close to Makil as if to steady the other should he need support, and behind them both Borkin and Eban whom Thora had last seen in the fortress of the valley heights. Makil carried the sword behind his shoulder and, though his face was very gaunt, he seemed to walk well—as if some surge of renewed life had cured him of the weakness she had seen in him.

As the valley party advanced Thora, feeling foolish, arose from behind her rock. The four men looked from her to Tarkin and there was wonder in their faces, as if they might have expected to catch up with her but not in such company—that they found Tarkin's presence confounding.

Malkin and the male took running leaps to cross the stream and pelted forward to clasp hands with Tarkin, their hissing speech low and eager. Then Malkin went back to Makil where the men were wading the shallow water, and the male joined Eban. If they communicated with their blood-brothers Thora did not hear or understand. Only Makil's look of astonishment grew and he surveyed measuredly at Thora.

"You have been to the Wood—" The wonder in his expression was repeated in his words. Borkin gave a sudden jerky movement as if he would repudiate that.

Was it, Thora's antagonism roused again, that he believed no female dared meddle in such matters as this of the blood-sisters—

brothers? That the furred ones could only company with men?

"I go where the Lady would have me," she retorted sharply. "I have met with Tarkin and we understand each other—and that there is that we must do, blood-bond or no."

"But you are not sister-blood," Eban said slowly.

"All roads are not the same, even if they lead in a common direction," Makil said before the girl could answer. "She has been accepted by our little ones after another fashion. There is nothing for us to question if the Folk have already decided it so. It is only good that we can be as one in the matter now before us."

As one? Something within Thora queried that statement. "Not yet do I say that, Makil of the Sword. I owe a debt to you perhaps. To these others of your kin I owe nothing. What I do is because the Lady wills it—not through or by any command issued from this Hunter Priest of yours." She favored Borkin with a glance which perhaps he did not see, but which measured the man she still distrusted and would continue to, until she was sure that he would not try again to use her for his own purposes.

They would join against the common enemy because that was willed. However that did not mean that she surrendered any part of her will or talents to any except the Lady!

Thora speedily discovered that these valley men were trained in the art of journeying across open land with as little exposure of their presence as possible. She thought that she had learned much of such sulking during her own wandering, but these four and their furred companions were masters of such craft. Kort fell into his old role of scout —ranging ahead. And even Borkin came to grudgingly admit that the hound served better than any spy they had previously employed.

They used every scrap of cover which a zig-zag path afforded them. It was plain that, away from their own valley, none of her new companions held anything in trust. When they camped at night they chose cover carefully, and always they headed westward—but now their direction angled also south toward the river up which she had come with Malkin.

It was not only against any who might sight their passage by day that they guarded. Each night Borkin and Makil followed a ritual about their campsite, setting up a barrier of force. Makil unsheathed his sword, and, with its point, drew lines in sod or soil. Borkin recited words, of which Thora only recognized a few. This done the travelers seemed at greater ease, though she noted they still kept watch by lot and were alert to anything which might move in the dark.

12

The men from the valley were a silent lot, or
perhaps they were chary of words because
they found Thora too strange to hold in trust.
She could not tell which motive kept them
largely without speech save for very necessary
remarks. The furred ones hiss-whispered
among themselves from time to time, but if
they shared any thoughts with those two they
were blood-bound to, the girl could not detect
it. At first she was willing to be as uncommuni-
cative in turn.

On the third day she began to tire of this continued silence, was no longer willing to rest on
her pride and wait for them to explain where
they went, or what they sought—besides their
missing comrade. Though she did believe that

it was Karn's capture which had partly brought them into this debatable land.

Still Thora studied eagerly the land they traveled through, hoping to spy some landmark out of her vision. But perhaps because that had been taken in complete darkness any such were not disguised. At last she addressed Borkin directly, determined that, since he was so obviously her unfriend here, he was the one to be approached first. The most difficult must always be assailed from the beginning—the greater trial before the easier one.

"You seek a place of the Dark Ones—" That could be either a question or a statement. "What trail do we follow to find such?"

He glanced at her with no warmth, only a frown of impatience.

"We cannot find them. With fortune perhaps we might sense one of their trails. But we can more readily seek what they want most. Then, seemingly as far as they can know—we can betray our presence in our excitement. Having thus broken our own defenses, they will speedily come seeking us—"

It was as she had suspected, they believed (as she also had been taught) that those of the Dark could detect any use of power within a land they knew. But what did *they* seek—besides valley men for prey? She opened her mouth to ask that and then understood—the storage place in which she herself had already found the dead Dark One and those he led!

That must be where they were headed now—to set bait in a trap the Dark could not resist.

Thora thought of the rat things they had fought there during their own escape—and of what secrets unknown, unlearned, might lie waiting for the uncovering. One might easily so loose more than could be controlled. Now she looked from Borkin to the other three and found them watching her—Borkin and Eban narrowly, Martan and Makil more openly.

"Do you believe, Borkin," she asked deliberately, "that those who stored their things of knowledge left no safeguards? It may be that both you and the Dark Ones will find more than you bargain for—"

"You speak," Makil broke in, "always of 'you', as if *you* have no part in this, Chosen. Still you continue to walk our way and the sister," he indicated Tarkin where she stood a little apart with her own kind, "travels it with you and says that a task has been laid upon you."

"Perhaps that is so. I am willing to walk your trail and wait to see what is required of me—but not by you." Her chin arose a little and she held herself very straight. "That we have a common enemy binds us. Yet we have not drunk Friend-cup, nor are we kin-named. I do not know why I have been sent, only there is HER purpose to be served. That is sufficient for a Chosen. In HER own time She will call me. Yet what lies in the place you would invade—that is not of Her—nor perhaps even of such power as we could wish to use. To meddle there may be a costly mistake."

Makil shook his head. "We do not meddle; we shall use it for bait. The matter lies as Borkin says. Those of the Dark hunt such caches. Let them know that this one is found and they will pour forth from their lair. Thus can we learn where that lies and perhaps more of the full weight of what is ranged against us. For a find such as Malkin has spoken of is a mighty matter—perhaps it would even bring their chief out to view it."

They came to the river—and then the dead tree where Thora had been moved to hang the tattered cloak of evil. Of that there remained no sign, save there were prints on the ground about the shattered trunk, the marks so overlaid that one could not sort out any of one definite pattern.

Martan went down on one knee to study these closer. Then he held out a finger, moving it back and forth, as if trying to outline the half seen. Yet never did he touch the disturbed earth itself. As the younger man drew back, Borkin closed in, holding in one hand a small bag of the same dark green material as their clothing and which bore on its sides the silver marking of the spiral. Out of it he took a pinch of coarse grained stuff like silver sand, and, with a practiced swing of his wrist, he sent that flying out to form a spiral on the ground, covering those unreadable tracks.

It was as if he had sown fire instead of dust. For there arose from the center of the spiral a puff of smoke no larger than Thora's little finger. That traveled along the length of the spiral outward until it reached the very end of the line. For a second or two it hung so—then its tip dropped—pointed—before it was gone and the spiral which had given it birth also faded away.

"West," Martan stood, his hands on his hips, staring over the level lands. Nothing lay there—-only in a far distance some dark blots moved slowly—grazing beasts Thora believed. Still she guessed that what Borkin had just done was not because they truly wanted to know in what direction the Enemy had gone, but rather he had deliberately induced his first troubling with Power—one which should be quickly picked up by any watching for just that.

From that time on they traveled by night, their camps as hidden as they could make them. Makil took greater care with the invisible guards he put about each. Thora now understood that it was a race with time to find what they sought—that crevice leading into the ancient storehouse where they proposed to set up their trap.

Doubts hung heavy in her mind though she did not voice them. Four men—and a Chosen without full training—three of the furred ones whose abilites and talents might be great but of whose strength she was ignorant. So small a band—and what could the Dark hurl against them? She thought of the night-black citadel into which she had gone in vision and, though she had seen but few there, that did not mean the Dark Ones could not summon perhaps as great a following as the raiders who had so easily overrun the Craigs. They must have a vast belief in themselves, these valley men. Or else they were desperate in their taking of chances. That she had become a part of this— Inwardly she continued to wonder at the folly of her presence here, and then was a little frightened at such rebellion against what must have led her to this band.

Lying in hiding during the day, Thora slept only fitfully. Kort ranged farther and farther. Sometimes they did not see him from dawn to dusk. Always when he returned he brought prey with him, rabbits, large birds of the open country who were poor flyers.

Malkin and Raskin, the male, had what remained of the vials from the cavern. In addition they drank the blood of such offerings as Kort brought. But they were also nourished otherwise, and Thora, seeing what they were given by their chosen companions, found it distasteful, that bond even more one to be questioned by one of her own kind.

For each morning Makil and Eban moved aside heavy bands they wore on their wrists and reopened small cuts from which the furred ones sucked for the space of a breath or two. Such small tastes apparently were worth more to Malkin's species than any other food, and they needed but little of it.

Though Thora could not have found her way back to the crevice, Kort and Malkin together were able to do so. They came at dawn to that black slit which she had no wish to enter again, but down which she had no choice but to go. They were alert for the rats in the dark but the men produced from their packs sticks, the tips of which had been dipped many times to build a thick coating of a hardened green substance. They peeled the covering from one of these and set it alight. Borkin carried it into the crevice and the torch was strong enough to reveal every detail of the slit through which they went, Kort, growling, his back hair raising, walking stiff-legged back to the scene of their own battle.

The vanquished enemy was revealed shortly by a huddle of bones already picked clean of even the last tufts of hairy skin. Eban bent closer to look at the skeleton.

"The great rats, yes. Eaten by their own kind, doubtless. But larger even than any we have seen before."

There were three more such skeletons. Then there came a faint squeaking from a break in the wall at the level of their heads. But none of the creatures of the dark ventured out into the light of the torches, so their party made their way on without any attacks. Twice they paused for Makil to face the back trail, to touch sword point to rock on either side. Not in a protective pattern this time, Thora was sure, but rather to set deliberate guides for those who might follow.

But surely those of the Dark forces would not be so lacking in cunning as not to suspect that this might have been done on purpose? Perhaps that thought of hers showed in her face, for Makil, allowing the rest to get a little in advance, said in a low voice:

"We do not underrate those we go against, Chosen, even if it seems thus to you who knows not our ways. In the past, before the Dark arose to be such a danger in these lands, it was always our custom to mark trails so—especially if they might lead to some discovery of the Days Before. Then those summoned to help us explore could find our path quickly. The Dark may well believe now that we are so avid for what we seek that there will be other parties of our people following and that these marks are left for them. Also they have that pride which is the cloak of their belief in themselves and contempt for us. It is very common for them to judge that we are less than ground-crawling insects which they can easily crush beneath a boot sole.

"They have swept far and fast during the past four years, and I think that they may have begun to believe that there is nothing and no one who cannot be bent to their purposes. Unless," and now he looked at her very searchingly "—unless they have been alarmed since you faced their leader in his own foul chamber."

"From which," Thora immediately pointed out, "I would perhaps not have come forth again without your aid. Do not build too much on any power of mine—for I was the least of the Circle Servants in my own place, being only one who waited to be raised to full power."

"Still you possess what they have not faced before—at least among us," he continued. "Do not cry down what you have to offer. The People," he made a slight gesture to where Malkin pattered before him, "are never wrong in their weighing of our potentialities. That Tarkin accepted you, and without forging any blood bond, is a new, strange thing—so it means much. You do not have the People among you?"

The girl shook her head. "No. And in our legends familiars are said to be servants of the Dark—though when I met with Malkin, my Moon jewel told me that this was not so. But your bond with them is one I cannot share—" Perhaps a shadow of distaste crossed her face then for he was looking at her very soberly.

"Yes. The paths we walk are divided. But for the present it is enough that those run side by side forward to a common end. I think that you feel Borkin is difficult to deal with, but among us he is a 'Chosen' also."

"But you," Thora was moved to say then, raising her hand to indicate his sword, "are perhaps more than Borkin. What is this Weapon of Lur," she remembered what he had named it, "which you carry to such purpose?"

"It is a focus of the Power, even as is your own jewel. No, I am not greater than Borkin. He is much more learned in the old rites than any now among us, save for those who have withdrawn and meditate away their day and nights in the High Hall—where he in time shall also take his place. But, as with you, we have our Chosen. It happens that in this generation I am the only one who can lay hand to the Weapon—so I became its servant. To carry it is no easy task—and one no man would wish because of ambition. It lays many bonds upon its bearer and his life becomes wholly that of Lur."

In the torchlight his gaunt face showed the hollowing of cheeks, the setting of lips, marking one who had long borne a heavy burden and learned endurance as a deep and bitter lesson. Thora knew a stir of awe when she looked upon Makil, whereas Borkin, for all his vaunted power, aroused in her only opposition and dislike. Martan, the Windrider, she felt she understood—in spite of her wonder for the art he had mastered which made him free of the air. He was not unlike a young man of the Craigs—one of those restless seekers from whose ranks the Winter Hunter was usually drawn—men who were not content with flocks, herds and fields, but needed a different way of life.

Eban, she did not know beyond the fact that he seemed of consequence to the valley's defenses. But Makil was a different type of man, new to her. In him she sensed things which she might never understand were they to travel in company for their lifetimes. She discovered that she no longer held any shadow of resentment toward him, not merely because he had brought her out of the Dark with his mysterious weapon, but because he was what he was. She would like to know him better, for he presented to her a mystery—though she doubted that even were she to appeal to the Lady would she ever be able to solve such.

They scrambled down shortly into the great spread of the underground storage place and came to that party of the dead led by the ancient enemy. Borkin stooped close over the form of the Dark Master which was so well covered by the folds of the cloak upon which time had seemed to have no effect. Having inspected the body very closely as it lay he stood to rummage in his pack and finally brought forth a well-polished length of wood which was pure white for half its length, a deep and lustreless black for the rest.

The black tip of this he inserted very carefully under the outflung edge of the cloak. With a sudden movement of his wrist, heaved the folds up and back to reveal the inner side. This was, as Thora had expected, covered thickly with those same symbols she had seen on those worn by the Enemy in her vision. Some of those metallic-hued designs made her queasy, so blatantly foul were they. Still Borkin studied them intently as if their meaning was such he must learn more and more, in spite of their vicious evil. Again and again he lifted, pulled, twisted at the cloak until they could finally see the body it had covered.

The limbs were now only bone beneath a covering of dark, dried skin—still somehow the corpse did not look as dead as those among which it lay. Thora shifted uneasily, though she would not allow herself to move away. She tensed—there was something like a wind touching her—save this was within and not outside the envelope of her body. She pulled free her spear, half expecting to see those limbs twitch, the thing strive to rise.

Kort crouched beside her snarling, fangs bared. It would seem that he shared her feeling. While Tarkin crowded in upon the girl's left, her eyes ablaze. Thora saw a flame in the air which was not from the torch which they no longer needed in this grey lit place. Makil had his sword out and in the hilt—for he gripped that weapon now by its blade, the jewel crystal began to glow. Suddenly—

She had not been mistaken in her fears. One of those skeleton legs had drawn up a little, not shifted by Borkin's moving of the cloak which had covered it. Yes, it was drawing up—!

"Back—all of you!" Makil ordered. Thora's hand gripped the spear, ready to stab.

Borkin leaped away, so quickly that he tottered, not quite sure of his balance. That which was under the cloak heaved, started truly to rise. But from the crystal of the sword hilt shot a beam of light which was like that she had seen in her vision of the crossroads. It struck full upon the dead-alive thing.

Still partly hidden by the cloak, that writhed. Not here, but far away as if that which gave it life was at a distance, the girl heard a cry of rage and agony. The cloak charred, giving forth a vile-smelling black smoke. Flame ran back and forth across the material, leaving only ash behind. As the burned fabric fell away, the noisome thing beneath it struggled a little before it followed the cloak into ashes. Still that residue lay in a distinct pattern on the floor, forming the outline of a nude body, not the near-skeleton they had seen when Borkin had begun to uncover it—but rather as if what had been destroyed was full fleshed.

Now the light of the sword swept up and down its length. There came a gleam from the pavement, reddish, as if there were coals there still sullenly alive. From head to foot Makil pointed the beam—then back again, until there was nothing left—not even the powder of the ashes.

"They know now—surely—" Eban commented as they stood staring at the stretch of flooring on which now an already fading stain marked the ancient death.

"Yes," Borkin agreed heavily, "there was a linkage. They might have already been seeking, and what there remained of this one of them was enough to draw their power. He must have been a great master of evil in his time."

"But—" Thora paused, ran her tongue over lips which were suddenly dry, "that—that thing could not have been alive!"

"It was not. However, with a linkage another will could animate it for a moment. It might have done even more, had there been time and opportunity. I would say—" Borkin glanced about at the dim stretch of pillar framed aisles, "that it will be well for us to search this place carefully. If, by chance, another such as this one lies here—" He shook his head.

"That is well said!" Martan agreed. "I would not have thought that they were so powerful. After all we have been many years—generations—learning what we can do. This awakening of the dead is a powerful ensorcellment indeed. How much else may they have to draw upon?"

Eban shrugged. "It is enough that they have any. But at least for now we have put an end to this particular game. Also our purpose is in part accomplished, when the master who strove to work his black art here met Lur's light he, himself, may have left this place of existence. Defeated spells can recoil threefold or more on those who launch them. However, his hounds will be out now, roused to the hunt. I would suggest we learn all we can in as short a time as possible—we may not go undisturbed for long."

Thus once more Thora paced between the rows of boxes and containers—up one long aisle and down the next. There was little to be seen save that which was so carefully storaged. Though, when they reached that place where she and Malkin had camped, the furred people scattered, seeking other containers of the blood powder, seizing eagerly on more vials after Eban had taken the tight lid off a cylinder they pointed out. They stored their prizes in a large bag Malkin swung from one shoulder.

Kort ranged here and there, sometimes wedging his massive body through narrow spaces, to go sniffing along high piles. Then they came to the bulky things covered with the thick fabric. The valley men, Martan in the lead, cut the lashings on a couple of these and pulled away lengths of the protections, to uncover what were not unlike massive wagons of a kind Thora had never seen. Martan, eagerly crawling up, around, and over these, announced that he was certain they had once been fashioned to travel across land, even as the wings had been meant to aid man into the sky. But there was no way he could see to bring these to life again.

Yet Martan continued to look back at them wistfully as they moved on, and Thora believed that he wanted more than anything a chance to master one of those strange metal monsters and make it serve him even as it has served men of a near-forgotten time.

Why had these been left here so protected, she wondered? Were they intended to carry away the other materials stored here? Were they to transport people? Or were they really weapons of some kind—stored ready for other raiders to carry red ruin across the land? Had those Before had such deadly enemies? No one might ever know now. Whatever purpose they were left here to answer would go now forever undiscovered.

The size of this place amazed her more and more. They discovered again the sentry at his everlasting watch, found that other door through which Thora, Malkin and Kort had come—continued past and on. The length of the shadowed cavern-hall was almost beyond their reckoning and they came to a stop at last,

tired and hungry, to rest among the boxes, so
awed by the mere sight of all this hidden store
of the unknown that they spoke very little.

Kort had vanished and Thora grew worried.
There were the rat things— Did those come inside? Also, though they had found no more evidence of any invasion by Dark forces, they had
not explored completely. And every time she
thought of that body which had tried to rise,
imbued with false life, she shivered. Tarkin
laid her hand gently on the girl's arm and
looked up into her face.

"The dead—they are gone—"

"But you saw—what if the power might
use—others—so?"

Just as she spoke there rang out a furious
barking, a sound which was both a challenge
and a warning. Kort's alert brought them all to
their feet, facing toward the other end of the
high chamber—to where they had entered and
the Weapon of Lur had proven its power.

13

Thora began to run, taking no heed of the others. In spite of the distortion caused by echoes, she was sure of her goal. Kort's clamor meant there was danger, something very much to be feared. She began to school her first unthinking response into more fruitful caution, not cutting the speed with which she ran, but rather watching ahead for any cover which the storage might provide. She watched, too, for any shadow or movement which might have no place there, ever glancing overhead now and then. The valley men had wings—though those could not have been used here. But who knew what surprises the Dark Ones might have uncovered when there was need? However all she sighted was the grey form of one of the furred people who had clambered up to the top of those piles of boxes and was running along there even more swiftly than she.

The advantage of an advance aloft caught Thora's instant attention and she took precious moments to mount a stairway of containers and follow (with leaps between piles) the same path. Just as quickly as it had begun, Kort's warning was cut off.

Had he been killed? Thora choked down, brought under control, her instant flare of rage at that thought. This was no time to allow emotion to cloud her judgment, hamper what skills she had so painfully learned.

The furred one ahead (though the light was dimmer here aloft)—she was sure that was Tarkin. But this was no easy road. Many times Thora went to her hands and knees, not daring to look down as she balanced on one pile or another, lest she be forced into a misstep. Nor did she glance back to see if the valley men followed. Kort was not their comrade—they owed him nothing. They might even consider, that, for the success of their own mission, they should sacrifice the hound—or her. She still mistrusted Borkin, at least, if it came to a matter of such a choice.

She reached the end of the long aisle and could see, across a wide space of open, the wall of the cavern hall. Yes, it was Tarkin who crouched there before her. And to their right, not too far away was the muddle of the dead.

To the left—

That direction looked oddly murky, more shadowy, as if whatever source lighted this place had begun to fail or had been deliberately tampered with. And it was from that direction, the girl was sure, Kort had sounded his alarm.

She hesitated and then forced herself to jump to the next pile in the companion aisle to the one down from which she had come. But she was too uncertain of her footing to leap a wider space now before her though Tarkin sailed across with ease.

Instead she must cross at floor level, and, since to descend and mount thus at every aisle would only waste time, Thora scuttled across the pavement. She had thus passed the mouths of two more aisles when a stench clogged her nostrils, bringing acrid bile into her throat. If evil could be distilled as the Craig women distilled the scents of herbs and flowers to make sweet their homes and their persons, this was then its very essence.

Fighting down nausea, Thora slowed pace. That smell was a warning enough. It would not do for her to plunge blindly on into the midst of what might be a band of well-armed enemies—those who controlled in addition unknown forces.

Reaching down, she caught at the gem which she had brought into the open after their encounter with the unquiet dead. The

stone was warm in her hand, and not because
her touch had made it so. A single glance was
enough to show it was glowing. Hastily she
grasped it tightly, her fingers hiding that
gleam, feeling confident that those she went to
face would be warned by their sensing, if not
by sight of it. Then she strove to order and
quiet her own thoughts, to build a wall behind
which to imprison emotion. So she might go
into battle with all the strength of will she possessed.

Tarkin had not descended from her more
lofty path, being able to make easily the leaps
which carried her from one line of storage
containers to the next. Now the furred one
paused and with a wide sweep of her arm,
signalled to Thora. Unwillingly the girl
pressed against the next barrier of boxes,
while the furred one swung down until her
head was not far from Thora's.

Her hissing speech was no louder than the
faintest of human whispers. Though any
sound in this heavy silence seemed so acute
that Thora had even limited her breathing to
the most shallow and lightest of gasps—still
fearing that that might be heard.

"Near—up!"

Another wave of the claw hand. Tarkin scuttled back to the top of the box wall. Thora,
gripping the haft of her spear between her
jaws with a pressure which made them ache,
followed her up, to lie belly down on the perch

and survey what lay ahead.

At first she could see nothing of Kort. But there were indeed others there. The sight of them froze her, sent her again striving to regulate her breathing.

She counted some ten men—not red robes —but men, such as she had seen among the river pirates. Save that these wore—like the valley men—a single form of garment—not odds and ends of looted clothing. That garment—a grey-brown in color not unlike Tarkin's fur—so melted into the shadow which appeared oddly thick here, that, if it was not for their movements and glimpses of their very white faces, she would not have been able to distinguish them. For many of them wore coverings also over their head—not the hoods of cloaks—but rather mufflings which left only a portion of their cheeks and chins showing—the rest being holed for their eyes.

Three well to the fore had doffed those head coverings, revealing only bleached white skin—as if they wore skulls upon their shoulders. Even the tops of their heads sprouted no hair, and their features were odd in cast, possessing an indefinably alien aspect. Thora could not explain that difference—she only knew it existed.

Their eyes were so large and sunken, that, at first glance, one might believe the bony sockets empty pits within the planes of those skulls. The noses were long, thin, and sharp at the tip, not unlike avian bills in contour, while the mouths those noses overhung were wide and very thin-lipped—the lips so dark in color they might have been stained with clotted blood—looking far more like unhealed wounds than normal features.

Each was so like his fellows that all three might have been brothers, of a single family. And, as they stood there, a little apart from their companions, they kept gazing about, the three heads sometimes jerking sharply from left to right and back again, as if they were impatiently waiting for someone else to arrive.

At length Thora located Kort. The struggles of the hound had rolled his body over close to the base of the very pile of boxes on which she now crouched. He was looped around and around with a black cord which showed starkly against the lighter fur of his belly and Thora saw that a couple of strands had been drawn about his muzzle so that he could not open his mouth, though he still writhed and fought against his bonds.

One of the waiting unmasked glanced at the helpless hound and uttered a grating sound which Thora thought might be laughter. He made a slight hand gesture and the nearest of the masked men strode to Kort's side to plant a boot into the hound's ribs, sending him slamming back against the stacked boxes.

Thora's grip on her spear was so tight that

her fingers ached. But she had only that and
her knife, and the enemy were too many to attack blindly. To be captured herself would not
help Kort and might well be the end of the trail
for them both. To fall into the hands of the
Dark Ones did not only mean perhaps torment
and bodily death, but worse—an entrapment
of the spirit—perhaps just such as they had
tried on Karn in their own citadel.

Still the girl was very aware that the callous
cruelty of that blow, had, in a small way, been
a favor. Now the girl looked to Tarkin, edging
closer to the furred one. The murky light here
was so great a disguise for that small, slim
body that surely Tarkin and the advantage
over those below.

The furred one's hand flashed out, claws
closed about the hilt of Thora's precious knife,
then Tarkin nodded downwards. Did she believe she could so loose Kort? And, once being
loose, might not the enraged hound betray
them by attacking at the men? Thora had no
sure way of communicating now with Kort. So
she gripped tight Tarkin's wrist when her
companion would have unsheathed the knife.

The furred one jerked back impatiently.
With her other hand Tarkin pointed to the
men, shaking her head so vehemently it was
plain that she believed any chance to free Kort
must be made immediately. Reluctantly Thora
allowed her weapon to be drawn. Then Tarkin
slipped away across the boxes, moving like a

shadow among a haze of shadows—this with the ease of one who might have done this many times over.

She dropped to the floor, disappeared into the well of the dusk which held Kort. He who had laughed at the struggles of the hound impatiently waved a hand. His force appeared alert to the silent command. They melted away—vanishing as quickly and quietly as Tarkin had, perhaps only into hiding where Thora could not detect them.

Into the space where they had stood only moments earlier strode another small party. Here came the glow of a red cloak, the cloth of it seeming to radiate, so that he who wore it carried with him a nebula of bloody mist. He, too, went bareheaded and Thora, with a thrill of what she honestly admitted to herself was fear, recognized the Dark One she had confronted in that other place.

What was so important as to bring him? Did the Dark Ones believe that in this place lay some potent weapon or piece of knowledge which was worth the personal attention of one of their major leaders—so that he had come himself in search of it? Or was it that he had been drawn here by the arrival of the valley party, feeling so secure that he did not have to fear attack? Or was there, too, another possibility—that the red cloak lords, in spite of all their powers, did not trust their underlings? Perhaps it was a combination of all these which had produced this more formidable opponent now.

He stared about him with an arrogant air, not speaking to the waiting men, rather ignoring them completely as if it were his decision alone as to the worth of what might lie here, as if his eyes could pierce each container or box and instantly be aware of the value of its contents. While the unmasked trio, impassive as to countenance, retreated, to stand with the two others who had followed him, leaving the fore field free to their commander.

One of those who had followed him here was a blind drummer. His bare body was crossed by a wide sling to which was attached a drum—neither that tall one, nor the bowl shaped one, which her spear and knife of vision had shattered. This was a cylinder, resting near his hip to one side, and he constantly smoothed the skin of it with his fingertips, producing a low humming not unlike the sound an insect might make. His blind eyes were wide white spheres, and his head was a little atilt as if he listened for something which other ears might not hope to catch. His companion was—

Thora sucked in her breath before she mastered her surprise. She had seen the furred ones—who her people did not know, and those legions of the Red cloaks, who were foreign to the country of the Craigs. Doubtless the western lands held other life strange to those within their own boundaries, and largely discounting the tales of the traders.

What this was—and it was NOT a human, of that she was sure—she could not have said. In the first place she would have believed it would have been more likely to go forefooted because of its shape, yet it padded along on its wide-clawed hind feet, its sinuous body topping the shoulder of the drummer, the front paws dangling against its belly. And those paws were very close in general shape to hands. The head was long and so narrow it seemed merely an elongation of the thick neck. This it swung from side to side, as it also shifted its weight from one foot to the other, while the lips of its pointed muzzle were wrinkled back in an ever present snarl.

The eyes in the head were small but, as with the furred ones, they showed highly luminous—being of a sickly yellow-green. While the fur or hide which covered it was patched with black, gray and yellow splotches in a wild profusion which appeared to make some portions near invisible in this dull light, other parts stood out clearly.

However, the worst of it was the aura of intelligent malignancy which hung about it, even as the red cloak hung about its master. Not only was it utterly vicious, but that viciousness was twined with an alien cast of mind which threatened a new danger.

Instinctively Thora pressed her moon gem

to her breast as she had from the moment the Dark Lord and his two companions had come into sight. Now she felt the blaze of warmth in her talisman. Only a near source of great Power could have brought such response from the gem.

Still the cloaked leader stood unmoving, only his eyes traveled over what lay before him. Then he gave a single curt nod. As if he had been able to see, the blind drummer left off his humming strokes, now brought his fingers sharply down in a quick pattering of taps which sounded almost like words spoken in an unknown tongue.

And—

He was answered! Thora half-slewed about on her perch, a sharp fear stabbing at her. For those drum notes came from behind, from out somewhere along those many aisles. Kort must have run into only one party, while the rest of the enemy were exploring the chamber in greater force, setting up a net to capture those who had invaded it before them.

It was the Dark Lord's turn to stand with head slightly atilt, listening to that return of drum roll. That he had sent a message and was receiving one in return was surely true. Thora wondered if she dared move, try to retreat back over the boxes.

It was the monstrous animal thing which moved first. Its head strained up a fraction higher, turned. Thora was sure that those yellow eyes had somehow fastened on her—that she was as exposed to it as if she lay in the open under the bright sun.

From its gaping jaws came a low, hoarse cry. Then it threw its length forward. Only it did not strike upward towards where Thora lay her spear in hand—nor did it complete the attack it had so clearly intended. For it was met while still in mid-air by Kort who sprang in silence, with none of his usual growls or snarls—rather as if he was preserving every atom of energy to the matter of getting a deadly jaw grip on that serpentine form.

The hound had closed fangs on one of the short forelegs, throwing the creature off balance and bearing it down on the pavement. Then Thora felt Tarkin move back up beside her. The girl caught at the down covered shoulder so close to her own, drew the furred one close, so that her lips brushed the other's cheek as she whispered urgently:

"Can you get away—warn the others?"

Tarkin nodded, slipped out of Thora's hold, slid backward along the boxes. With the furred one on her way, Thora's full attention returned to the fight. She had expected the men to take a hand, but they stood watching as if in their minds there could be no possible doubt as to the outcome.

Both hound and monster were bleeding. The monster kicked out with powerful hind feet as it rolled upon its back, striving to tear Kort's belly open with one of those well directed blows. But the hound fought with all the cunning of years as a hunter and a trail rover. He had loosed his first hold, leaving the small upper limb limp, the bone plainly crushed, and now made quick rushes, scoring many times on the blood spattered, spotted hide. Whenever the creature strove to use its injured limb it squalled—though Kort, far from his usual custom, continued to fight in complete silence.

That none of the men had shown any surprise at the appearance of Kort, who they must have thought to be a helpless prisoner, was first a source of amazement and then one of growing unease for Thora. Once more the Red Cloak gestured and the drummer answered.

Those flying fingers which had sent out the message were now changed for the heels of his hands, which he brought down, his palms a little cupped, on the surface of his instrument. The resulting sound was so deep, sharp—that Thora's hands swung to her ears, then she dropped the moon gem to its chain, and held on grimly to the edge of the box on which she lay.

For the beat had set her perch trembling, stirred the very air about, so that her body was being moved back and forth, as if she would be shaken from the height to the pavement below. Striving to hold to safety she was only partly aware of the influence those sounds had on the fighters, though she was startled alert to that by a cry from Kort—a wailing howl.

The hound swerved back from his prey, his head low, pawing frantically at his ears with first the right and then the left forefoot. Oddly enough the Red Cloak's own fighter was in no better case, for it rolled squealing, hammering its head up and down on the pavement, as if it had suddenly gone mad.

It twisted its body, sending blood spattering outward from the injured forepaw—some drops even falling on the drum head as the creature dug its powerful hind feet into the flooring, its head darting up now toward the drummer himself though the blind man did not retreat from the threat the creature suddenly offered.

Thora had loosed her hold on the boxes because she must, or throw herself down mindlessly. She forced her fingers into her ears. The beat was now echoed throughout her whole body, her heart responding in a faster and faster thump of its own while she jerked and twisted, trying to control her limbs.

Kort howled again, a sound of despair and agony. Then, somehow, he edged his body around, leaped into the aisle, and ran as she had never seen him run before. Still the drummer beat while the others merely stood watching.

The heavy lids were dropping over the Dark Lord's eyes. He might be withdrawing so into some inner place which was so much his own that he was now heedless of anything about him. Thora shook and quivered. She could not hope to edge back along these unsteady boxes. Her poor head for heights had been enhanced a hundredfold. Now she dared only lie and wait, without hope, to be hurled to the floor, knowing that she was no match for any weapon such as this. In the dream vision she had sent the spear to attack the drum, in her present state she had no power of any concentration left in her.

On the pavement the creature still squalled and rolled. Still none of the men moved. The girl thought dimly once of those who had already withdrawn into the dusky aisles—perhaps gone seeking the valley men. But that fear was swallowed by her own present torment, in the thought that in a moment or two she would topple over—perhaps to fall directly to the feet of the Dark Lord.

Still the drummer kept to his body-shaking rhythm. Thora used all the strength she still possessed just to hold on. The leader raised his hand. In mid-note the drum was silent.

The girl lay weak and spent. She rested her head on her arm, unable now even to raise it high enough to spy upon those below. What other weapon would the Dark Lord decide to call upon?

When he struck she was more than half prepared for it. For she had long since acknowledged that nothing in her training had prepared her to face this kind of battle.

What reached for her was not a sound now—rather it was like the net which had held Kort at their coming. Not a visible one laid around her loop by loop. No, this was totally unseen, yet it held and compelled. Something—someone reached inside her—fastened upon the weakness the drum had awakened, turned her own lacks against her.

Her will was sapped, enmeshed, held captive—she could no longer fight. She might only answer to the pressure put upon her by he who had done this thing.

Thora wavered up. Her body, most of her mind (there was still a small portion which could only watch this action with desperate horror) was fully in subjection. Never in her life had she been so tamed, so beaten. This was worse than any defilement or maiming she could have imagined—this was a ravishing of an inner part of her, a reduction to degrading servitude.

She climbed down from her perch, walked into the open, to stand before the Dark Lord. The moon gem was blazing with bright power. Several times she had tried to break the bonds, to take the jewel into her hands to draw strength from it. But it would seem that the drum magic was supreme even over the gift of the Lady. Or else she herself was so sadly lacking in real courage she could not use that gift with true purpose. Thora remembered only too well how Karn had lain in that hall with the drums spinning darkness about him. That had been in vision—but this was real.

No expression crossed the Dark Lord's pallid face, nor did any of the unhooded men show surprise at her appearance. They might well have expected to have this prisoner so come freely into their hands.

Red Cloak's hand arose, he snapped his fingers as man might summon a hound to his will. One of the men strode to her, stooped, put out fingers to grasp the moon gem. That blazed a white fire, yet its radiance spread only a very little distance in the thickening murk. With a sharp exclamation the man jerked back. It was as if he had tried to draw a live coal from a blazing fire. Deep in Thora a small, very small hope stirred. The gem—yes, those were bonded only to her who used them with the Lady's favor. No one else might handle such unless it was during a rite and then only by the wearer's own wish.

For the first time the Dark Lord's lips moved as he spoke aloud:

"Throw that from you!"

Against every instinct, every small tatter of her old spirit, Thora's new slavery fought to obey his command. Her hand rose, fell, rose again— But when her fingers would have caught the gem, her will in battle against his compulsion, she cried out. Force turned strongly against her within her own body.

The Red Cloak held her gaze with his own half-hooded, gloating eyes. Now she believed she saw anger awaken within them. He pointed his index finger at her. From the tip of that shot a scarlet tongue of flame, searing her jerkin at the level of her heart, bringing tears of pain to her eyes.

"Off!" he cried, and there was something in his voice which was a faint echo of that enslaving drum roll. She knew that he would torment her truly unless she obeyed. And, by the Lady—she could not!

14

That hand of torment was rising again—the line of fire not so high, striking across the back of Thora's hand. A scream strangled in her throat. That part of her which the drum had not made prisoner strained, fought. She felt as if she were in the heart of a great whirlwind of force which was attempting to batter the life out of her. The pain in her flesh receded, she could not even see that face of evil before her. No, she was in the midst of a fire which leaped to utterly consume her—scarlet flames reaching out—around her there was only a thin, failing haze of defense.

Thora deliberately tried to forget her body, to batten down pain, and then fear. The gem—that was like the Lady's lamp at its most potent. There was no sky above her—so perhaps the moon power could not reach her in force. However, she opened her spirit, her mind to the fullest—knowing that she did so in great peril, for if this Dark Lord was indeed mightier than any force she could call upon, so could she give him full entrance.

Only what came to her was a drift of scent—subtle, floating, yet in truth cutting clearly through the stench of old evil—the scent of these flowers through which Tarkin had wrought her own night ritual. Then—

Into that part of her which Thora had deliberately opened flooded another, alien, mind, one which wove in and out, so sometimes the girl could grasp the edge of a thought and impression but never quite clear enough to fully understand. Save she knew that this was not of the Dark, nor was it of any force she had known all her life and had learned to use, after a half-crippled fashion.

There was something—something working here which was not of any world she knew! Something which had slept—or had been hidden for a long time—stirred. In part it was mated to that which was filling her, on another level it was totally strange. Yet she had opened herself to it and she was now an instrument of it, even as this Dark Lord would have made her a slave of his own force.

She heard—not such commands as he had been throwing at her—no, this came from much farther away. Partly it was conveyed by the hissing song of Tarkin and her People in the flowered place (for this new thing was of Tarkin); partly it was a sound of metal—-as if half a hundred swords such as the one Makil wore were being beaten threateningly against the floor on which they stood.

Thora could see again the steady movement of the drummer's hands beating out his monstrous rhythm. At the Dark Lord's feet crouched the beast Kort had fought, curled into a suffering knot of blood-stained fur.

Was she swaying, answering to the drum? Thora was not sure—for she was little herself, more simply a channel through which Tarkin (who—WHAT was Tarkin?) moved or worked other ensorcellments.

But the girl could move. Yes, her hands were free to clutch the moon gem. Not to seize it and throw it from her as the Red Cloak had ordered—rather to cling to it as the one point of safety in a wild world which she could no longer understand.

The Red Cloak—the hand he had raised to blast her was still outstretched, but it no longer beamed fire. His head tilted back a little on his shoulders and his eyes were totally closed. He, too, had withdrawn into his inner self.

For this moment Thora was no longer his prey. There was that approaching which he could not understand, against which his drummer had no power! The three men behind him drew back, their eyes aglitter, their heads snapping from side to side, as if they watched for something creeping upon them down the dusky aisles.

That scent of flowers, Thora drew a deep breath. No, the odor was not a true scent, even though the evil stench which appeared to hang about these Dark Ones was lessened. This was like a promise, a cord cast to rescue one who was being whirled away in a current strong beyond fighting. Thora set herself to concentrate upon Tarkin. Again the bond of the drum loosened a little—so she summoned up Power—

Power—YES! That was flooding into her hands, her heart, her mind! This was a place of long-leashed power. Not of the kind she had known, but of another sort. No moon gem, no Weapon of Lur could fight as this would do. Truly they, together, all of them, had summoned new strength out of the past—

For only an instant Thora's courage wavered. But Tarkin's essence, in spite of its alienness, was like a strong arm laid about her shoulders. She held the moon gem and waited.

At first the girl could believe that the hissing she heard was the voices of the furred ones magnified a hundred—a thousand times by some trick of this huge hall. Then, instead, she comprehended that this was another type of sound—that it was more closely allied to the metal clanking than it was to anything formed

within a humanoid throat. Above that came a
barking—a sharp frenzy which could only
have issued from Kort at the height of some
great excitement.

Those beats of the drummer were now
fainter, over-ruled by the other sound. She
could see that his cupped hands were pounding faster and faster—on his impassive, blind-
eyed face spread a slick of moisture. He was
putting into his beat more and more energy.
The monster which had been curled at the feet
of the Red Cloak raised its bloody head and
howled with a breaking cry. Then it whipped
around, gave a great leap as if it had been
driven to the very edge of endurance.

For a second of stark fear Thora thought it
had launched itself at her. There was a madness about it. Pink foam drooled from the corners of its mouth. But it flashed past her, heading down the aisle behind her. While the hissing there, the clanking, grew louder.

Past her shoulder shot a beam of white light.
That she recognized. It was born from the
Weapon of Lur. Its purity banished the murk
which seemed to hang about this section of the
hall where the Dark Ones had gathered. The
three behind the Dark Lord fell back, their
hands flying up, as if they tried so to ward off
some weapon. But, though the light caught the
Red Cloak full center, he still stood unmoving,
his eyes closed.

Thora saw his lips moving, twisting over

words. She knew he was evoking his own
power, pulling from the depths of his resources the full strength which lay in the
Shadow he owned as his inner master. The
cloak about him blazed, even as the eyes of the
furred ones caught fire when they were fully
aroused. His arms moved and the cloak
flapped wide, the symbols on its inner surface
appearing to twine and crawl—moving, she
knew not how, to shape and reshape, blazing
also to enforce the call which he was sending
forth.

The outer edges of that power touched the
girl, was like a mighty blow which sent her
reeling backward. Her body slammed against
one of the piles of boxes, and instinctively she
clung there, so keeping her feet. But that force
had not been aimed at her—no, it was still
undispatched—rather it was building within
him, being nourished, into greater growth, so
that at the moment of highest need he could
aim it, even as the beam of Lur's weapon was
used.

Also it would seem that what he garnered
formed a wall of defense about him. For,
though the light beam struck, it did not appear
to win through an ever-thickening scarlet
haze, given off by the cloak, to reach the man
who wore it. Now that spear of dazzling white
split, passing on either side of the Dark Lord.

Those behind him wailed, crumpled, as it
reached *them*. The edge of one shaft touched

the drummer on a shoulder. His arm fell limp and powerless to his side. Still he did not appear to know that he had been so partially disabled, rather he beat on.

Thora's head swung a fraction. She was released enough from the binding of the drum to be able to look for the source of the beam, that sound, Kort's own deep-throated barking. She saw—and could not believe what she saw.

Illusion—surely! She knew that this was no proper vision. Illusion so well spun that even with the moon jewel in her hold she could be bedazzled into mistaking shadow for substance—surely this must be true! Still it was so real—so plain—

Down the aisle advanced a massive crawling thing. On its back stood Kort barking. Beside him knelt Makil, holding up the weapon of Lur, high by its blade, in one hand, while with the other he kept tight grasp upon the monster he rode.

The creature of the Dark Lord leaped —straight for Kort. But it never reached the hound. Rather its bleeding body struck hard against the fore of the thing Kort and Makil rode. Striking so it fell. No paw reached out to beat it down, no fangs slashed from suddenly opened mouth to savage it, rather the body of the strange thing rolled on. There followed a sharp cry of agony as the beast was overrun, the heavy monster paying no heed to the thing it had crushed.

There came a spitting of flung darts from out of the shadows along the way. Those other followers of the Dark Lord must have lain in ambush there. There was even a bright burst of fire, but no weapon cut or singed the body of the thing which crawled ponderously forward.

Nor did any of those weapons reach the two on top of the thing's wide back. For there appeared to exist an invisible shield about them. A spear or two arched high, only to bounce back and fall to the pavement. Though that same defense was no barrier to the light of Lur's weapon but allowed the sharp beam through.

Thora flattened herself tighter against the box wall. Those who rode this monster might not see her—even Kort appeared to be looking straight ahead at the Dark Lord who still stood, his eyes shut, his whole being intent on what he would do. The surge of power which came from him was a searing wave and the girl clasped her gem tightly to her, sure that only it in her hands prevented her from now being shriveled into ash.

On rolled the monster. Thora glanced from side to side—first to its unrelenting advance, and then at the enemy. The three, who had backed the Dark Lord and commanded the early invasion forces, now lay on the ground, their bodies twisting, their hands over their eyes. The drummer was silent at last. He had crumpled at the very feet of his master, his blind face hidden where it rested on the drum he no longer beat.

Yet the Dark Lord stood, and his power waxed higher and higher. it was as if flames were running along his body, flaring upward from his cloak. Their tips reached forward towards the monster as his lips shaped words, which, to Thora, seemed to have substance, as if they issued forth in small puffs of evil black smoke. Still his defense held against the beam of the sword.

Now the monster was close and, for the first time, the girl suddenly realized that this was no thing with any life of its own. No, it was one of those metal made things which had been stored here—which was serving Makil now, as had the wings served Martan. In some manner the men from the valley had brought into half-life this thing, a servant of the Days Before. At the same time she sensed that against such as this no ritual of the Dark One could act, for a thing so fashioned possessed no mind, no essence of spirit which could be touched by power. It was no living animal, no man— nothing but lifeless material.

The thing was within touching distance now. Thora flattened herself yet more tightly against the box wall—fearing that she might be swept down, pulled under its bulk as had the hunting beast of the Dark Ones. She smelled—

Why did she still smell the flowers of the furred ones' dancing place? Why—?

Thora let out a cry and pressed the jewel so tightly in her hands that its plain silver rim of mounting cut into her flesh.

"Tarkin!" That name broke from her lips like a cry.

There was no answer in words. Instead a wave of reassurance, of comforting warmth. Kort and Makil rode this monster, but Tarkin—Tarkin was sending it to its goal!

Forward still it ground its way; the bulk of it passed Thora. She could see that it was like the one which they had uncovered in their search of this place earlier—save it was smaller. There was no sight of wheels such as a Craig cart possessed. Rather the thing might be sliding forward on its belly like a giant snail.

The waves of heat aroused by the Red Cloak were reaching such a temperature that Thora slipped back and away as best she could. Some of the boxes were beginning to char. She must get out of range of battle lest she be caught in this fire born of will—a thing which she could understand better than she could the creeping monster.

Lur's light still could not break through the Dark One's tight defense. The girl heard sounds among the boxes and stiffened. Out behind the monster stumbled those men of the Dark Force who had been set in ambush. They staggered from side to side, stumbling against one another, their eyes wide and unseeing. As if, by daring to attack the crawling thing, they had condemned themselves to blindness. Now followed a second crawler moving with the same ponderous pace, herding before it the men of the enemy. Among them a tottering second drummer his hands pounding steadily. On the back of this second machine rode Eban and Borkin. There was no sign of Martan, nor of the other furred ones. Nor could Thora see how the great machines were being driven.

One of the men behind the Dark Lord struggled to his knees and then his feet. He was crying out unintelligible words as he turned and wavered away, unsteadily, as if drained by some deadly wound of body. His two fellows still rolled on the ground, while the first drummer was entirely limp and unmoving.

The machine ground to a halt only paces away from the Dark Lord. Now, from oily beads which gathered on his forehead ran trickles of moisture. His body trembled, and Thora guessed that he had thrown into this battle the full stream of his life form. Still it would seem that the sword light could not break him. In her own hold the moon gem heated—built—

Thora now squeezed forward, not back. She edged along beside the crawlers, flinching from the heat of the attack-defense of the Dark

One. *That* she could understand, and in this moment perhaps she could play some small part at last.

She unhooked the chain which girded the moon gem to her body, allowing it to swing from those links of the Lady's own pure metal. This was no time for a spear, a knife, though it could well be time for an upsetting of two well balanced scales—She moved purely by instinct and that inner voice might be wrong. Thora only knew that she must try.

Holding the chain firmly by its free end, she swung the jewel back and forth, and then whirled it out towards the Dark Lord.

Those flames which encircled him, were fed by his knowledge, his spirit, touched the jewel. There followed a flare of such brilliance that Thora cried out, even though she had been shading her eyes with her other hand. Lur's Light drew upon that flare. So fed, it in turn pierced and struck!

The flames roared into an unholy fire, seeming to draw substance from the light of the sword. They hid the Dark Lord utterly by a wall which was first a sullen red, and then slowly lightened, to the yellow of the full sun—finally to the pure light of the sword beam, or of her own gem.

That which had been aimed had returned, a thousand-fold.

The column of flame, now purely white, began to shrink in upon itself, growing smaller and smaller. Thora waited to see the Dark Lord appear once again. But—

No one stood there secure in pride and power as the flames receded farther and farther. Was he kneeling? No, already the fire had shrunk—was he—?

There was nothing. Where the Dark Lord had wrought with the full command of the forces he could summon—there was nothing! Even the drummer who had lain at his feet was also gone. The flames in turn dwindled, died.

Now the two men left from the enemy force moved feebly, raised their heads. But there was no true life in them. They were as husks driven by the wind, allowed to fall where they might. Thora heard the other sounds, turned her head a fraction. Those who had been herded forward by the second crawler were falling—or blundering straight into the walls of the boxes, as if rendered mindless. The second drummer crashed forward—his instrument splintering under his body.

She believed she understood. In the final drawing-in of power the Dark Lord had pulled upon not only his own strength, but upon all the inner life of those who followed him. What were left now were bodies without spirit cores, bodies which were already beginning to drop to the floor, even the life of the flesh departing when there was no longer a true essence to hold it intact.

A vast weariness struck at her. Perhaps the Dark Lord had not made of her one of these husks, but he had pried and picked at her spirit. While, in the end, she had given all she had to give when she had used the jewel. Out of her, also had flown power, and, as Thora slipped down the side of the boxes against which she had leaned, she wondered dazedly if she were about to follow the Enemy into the final darkness.

That did not yet close about her. Makil and Kort leaped from the back of the monster, going forward into the battle field to survey those still remaining. Now the girl witnessed the opening of a lid pushed upward where the valley man and the hound had ridden into battle. Through that a furred body pulled itself.

Then, with a light leap, Tarkin also dismounted. But the furred one had no eyes for the site ahead. Instead she came straight to Thora, her clawed hands touching the girl gently, first on forehead and then over her heart.

Tarkin caught up the chain of the gem which was still between Thora's fingers, drew the silver length towards them. She touched the jewel itself with care, as if she expected to find it subtly changed in some manner, and then nodded as if reassured.

Moving quickly she laid the jewel on Thora's breast, just above the mark which the Lady had set upon the girl so long ago. There was no blazing heat in the jewel to wound and burn, but rather it was cool, as if Tarkin had dripped down upon her fevered flesh purest spring water.

The furred one again touched her gently. "Rest, sister—we have done much, but there is still more to do."

As if that were an order which she could not disobey, Thora closed her eyes, and then indeed swung into a darkness which was welcoming and in no way evil.

But it was a darkness in which there was life and movement—although none of it touched her. She was as one, who blind, still walked with sure, swift steps along a road where she knew she could not stumble and which would lead her straight to that which she had always sought.

Only she did not walk that road alone. There were many others, she could not see—carrying with them a sense of purpose and of need. So that Thora was sure that each had duty to perform. There was a feeling of time which—which was the road itself! That which lay behind ever gave birth to what lay still before. Far back there had been deeds done which were like unto the unopened buds of the flowers of the furred ones; now those deeds must open, then provide the final fruit.

Thora only trod that road for a heartbeat or so, but she knew it for the stream of true life, and that she was indeed a part of a weaving which had begun long before and was still to have its pattern finally set far, far ahead. The thread which was Thora had been pulled in and out—forming parts of many designs in passing—designs this Thora could not remember, for it was not the part of the thread to remember—unless that was allowed when one reached the destined end of the weaving.

She was now Thora, but she had been called by other names, and lived in different ways. All of those had had meaning and were of the power—though it might be a different kind of power. She had a flash of seeing—a Thora who went armed and who fought the Enemy—not a red-cloaked one—but of the same breed with weapons—who hurried with a fearful and pressing purpose to duty in a place where much must be hidden against another day—a Thora who had known during that journey the sharp outweaving of death—and then—

But that insight was only a flash and quickly gone. Yes, that which rested during the outweave could not be remembered. Perhaps the thread of those rested mindless and quiescent until it was time to help form a new design.

There was the scent of flowers—white bells of flowers. One danced among those drawing in strength—letting it flow out again as a balm and boon to others—

Thora felt a soft down against her cheek. She opened her eyes. Her head rested in

Tarkin's lap, there was the edge of a cup set to her lips, and the furred one was so urging her to drink. The red of the eyes above her was softly glowing—like the small flame of a trail side fire which was in its way a protection against all which might crawl in the dark.

"Drink, sister. This is now the time to be gone."

She felt the rough caress of Kort's tongue against the hand which rested at her side. The hound's bright eyes were watching her. Now he whined as she lifted that hand to lay upon his head. She drank and the liquid was sharp, aromatic. As Thora swallowed and felt it warm her, she knew also a return of strength so that she lifted herself out of Tarkin's hold to look around.

This was not the edge of the battlefield where she had fallen. They were in a wider, open space and before them on the wall was the outline of a door—a large door. There Martan and Eban were busied. The girl caught a glimpse of one of the same kind of wheels for locking as she had found in the tunnel leading to the place of storage—save that the door this one controlled was far larger.

There were the two crawling machines, also. Those two which must have brought the battle to the Red Cloak. Sitting perched on them by the open doors in the tops were Malkin and the male each licking from blood vials. As Thora moved Makil came quickly to her.

The Weapon of Lur was back in its sheath, its hilt showing above his shoulder. He was smiling, and there was a softening in his expression which she had not seen before.

"That was well done, Chosen," he said.

What was well done? For a moment Thora was confused. Then she understood and her hand sought her jewel.

"Better than that, even, Chosen. You brought us both the key and the lock, and now we shall see what comes of knowledge."

Thora shook her head— "I do not understand—" she began.

His smile grew wider. "Ask this sister," he nodded to Tarkin, "for indeed it was she who had the answers for us—"

15

This time Kort did not lead the way across the open land, rather it was Makil who walked at a steady pace, swinging the unsheathed sword above the quick growing grass. And sometimes from that grass, a stone, or even a spot of bare earth, there would shoot a spark of dull red—sullenly answering the Weapon of Lur, marking the path earlier taken by the forces of the Dark. He would rest at times, returning to ride with the others on those lumbering crawlers awakened from centuries old sleep. Then Borkin took his place, using the wand.

Thora rode reluctantly. She did not share the valley men's triumph at the new life of these massive things of metal. To her they were dangerous to her own kind and she placed no trust in them.

However, it had not been the men who had brought them to life. She discovered that when they began that journey and Martan spilled out eagerly all which had happened after she had run to Kort's call. Perhaps the machines had been made by people distantly akin to them, but it was the furred ones who actually controlled them.

That was almost the hardest to understand of all that had happened. Between such as Tarkin and these huge crawlers now trundling along Thora could see no kinship. Surely those who lived in the flower-entwined wood, and made magic akin to what she knew, could not be tied to this metal bearing—to her—the scent of dusty death. Her world was not the world of the storage place.

Surely it must have been men who had fashioned these things—men akin to that sentry they had first found dead. Martan, who gloried in his sky-conquering wings, he could be of the same distant blood. Why was not Martan then, or Eban, or even Borkin, the one to sit in that contained space where there was a board of many lights to be fingered—fingers used instead of busy and agile claws?

Yet it was Tarkin and Malkin who alternated in that cup of a seat there—by its size surely fashioned only for one of their race. And it was the male of their kind who guided the second of the moving boxes.

Thora could not believe that the furred ones had built these. She mulled over that mystery, as she held on firmly with both hands, set her teeth, gave care to maintaining her place on that tipping, rocking surface. Martan lay belly down on the second machine, his head hanging over the open door, his attention all for the actions of the driver. Eban was beside him on that second crawler, but appeared less concerned with how they were getting there, more with where they were going.

They crushed and battered a way onward. Nothing seemed able to deter the passing of these creeping fortresses of metal. They crunched earth, even small trees, under their treads—even as the one had overridden that monster of the Red Cloak.

Sometimes, as she so jolted along, Thora felt as if she traveled in a dream, even though they halted at intervals and she ate and drank with the others. She was still weakened by her struggle with the Dark Lord. Only the waxing moon overhead tied her to what she could understand. Here the Lady could be reached. They were the hunters, and that which Makil and Borkin could control pointed the path.

At the midpoint of the night they halted to camp. Thora climbed stiffly down from her perch, glad to stand on honest ground again. Borkin and Makil established the protection area, but not about the two crawlers—seemingly careful as they wrought so to avoid any contact with the machines. It was almost as if some half-forgotten enmity lay between the metal monsters and their own things of power.

She asked no questions, determined that she would keep herself aloof from what she distrusted so. This was not of the Lady—But then the valley men used the wings, thus it followed they were excited, pleased by the crawlers. This enthusiasm set them even farther apart from what she deemed right and natural.

Tarkin came to sit beside her. The furred one flexed the fingerclaws of both hands as if they had stiffened at their task. Then she dug into her food pouch and ate with noticeable appetite. It was as if—though to the eye she had only sat within that cubicle at the top of the machines and moved her fingers—she had performed some heavy, exhausting labor. Now she hissed a sigh, stretching her arms wide, straightening her back. Thora asked the questions which she would not voice to the men:

"Tarkin—what power do you use?"

The furred one's eyes were heavy lidded, they did not blaze—though the light in them was warm and steady.

"We have remembered—"

"Remembered what?"

"What was of old and who we are and why we were once born—through forces which were forgotten in the Change. We *were* born for a purpose, sister—though, in the long years since, we have changed also, becoming in many ways different from what we once were. Still in us there lay a deep memory asleep and it was wakened—perhaps by the power of that demon drumming. A forgotten place in our minds opened—" she shook her head slowly. "It is true that with us sounds have very great powers."

Thora remembered that pain-giving sound which Malkin had used to win their battle with the rats, and she could believe that. Also there was the dancing song. Yes, the furred ones had their own form of power—even as she her moon-call gem, Makil his sword, and Borkin that wand.

"So, suddenly remembering, we went to the task for which we were first intended, we brought out the machines which only we could move. In the Days Before there must have been some reason why we were the ones—" she rubbed her claws across her forehead— "but memory so deeply buried can be faulty. Perhaps my people never even knew why this task must be theirs. We were never like you—but that you already know. We spring from a far different seed, but we were given skills so we were used—"

"Used?" Thora repeated, that word had a sour taste in her mouth. To use intelligent life—that was of the Shadow, not of the Lady's clear way.

"Used!" Tarkin was firm. "It was the

Change which freed us, that we might learn what we ourselves chose to be, to grasp our own power. Still there was born into us—and that we could not forget—a need to be close to man—such as those of the valley. This bond became a different kind, perhaps, than it was intended—rather one of bloodsharing. Neither of us could understand just why we could and did make such a choice—why most of us had a longing to be so joined. I think it was another thing planned carefully by those who brought about our existence, so that in time of danger, the blood-bound could be ready to face danger as a single entity, one need, one mind— Save—" Now she looked directly at Thora, "when you came there was a new thing—a meeting between us which was not to be bound with blood. Perhaps this is a different pattern—a new one— But there is always a pattern."

Thora nodded. "Always a pattern," she agreed. "What is the true purpose of these things which you guide so?"

"They are weapons—such weapons as have not been seen—even in the Days Before, I believe. I think they were new made then, hidden for some reason—to be used only in some last battle. Just as we were raised and trained for that same warfare. They can and do carry death in a new and dreadful form, control powers which are not the kind we know—for they are neither of the light nor the dark, do not answer to words of ceremony, but can serve only those trained in their secrets. Now we take them to the Dark and with them," she spread her clawfingers wide, "we shall render such an accounting as perhaps shall banish the shadow. Maybe not forever, for that I believe cannot be done, but at least drive it hence for a space—"

Thora drew a deep breath. This was all like some wild trader legend. Still there stood the crawlers, and she had watched Tarkin make that mighty bulk answer to her as Thora's own knife and spear answered to the muscles of her body.

Surely this was an odd weaving, yet she could see how the strands had been gathered together—her discovery of Malkin—the finding of the underground storage place—then her journey to the valley—her own first brush with the Red Cloaks—her coming to the place of the furred ones and her meeting with Tarkin. Then came all the rest—the return for the treasures of the Days Before, the drums (which Tarkin believed reawakened memories) to teach the furred ones their once purpose in life— Yes, all was so well woven she could believe that this was how it was meant to be. What was the final design? The defeat of the Dark Ones with these forgotten weapons? It would seem that the furred ones and the valley men were united upon that. And she was still a part of it all whether she chose or not.

Awakening they moved boldly by day, crunching their way onward. Even in the sun, both sword and wand could mark for them the path along which the vanquished Dark Ones had come. Now Kort took to coursing ahead, adding his own senses to their seeking.

They had been two nights and a day on their way when, on the dawn of the second day, they saw ahead the rise of a dark mound, in the grey light that was familiar to Thora. This indeed was that place to which the silver footprints of her vision had led her.

The crawlers came to a stop and those riding leaped down. Then doors opened in the sides of the huge machines and they pushed inside —even Kort, coming at Thora's call, though he growled uneasily.

Within was a space as large as a small room, with stools fastened to the floor set at intervals. Before each of those wide murky plates on the wall. Thora seated herself cautiously, Kort on the floor beside her.

From somewhere came a bell note and that plate before her cleared into a window. She looked out at the dark side of that fortress.

Below each window a ledge jutted out from the wall, forming a half table above the knees of those seated there. On that surface lights began to play, shining faintly out of small pits the size and shape of a finger tip.

"Weapons controls?" Makil asked, not as if he were expecting any answer but rather musing on his own guess.

Lights as weapons? Thora could not see the connection—but then all of this was alien. She kept her hands firmly in her lap, resting by instinct over the moon gem.

That remained cold, lifeless. Now there was the prick of fear in her. But she must not allow that—must instead use her trained power to combat it. What—what if the Lady did not reach here? Thora was more lost within this rumbling box than she could be inside that threatening fortress ahead—for she had no control over any force now.

The girl shivered, longing to batter her way out of the crawler, but she was not even sure her legs would support her to the door. Her strength seemed draining along with her confidence.

Then, brighter even than the sun rising in the sky, a wall of flames leaped ahead of them. Sullen, blood red those were, giving off a black, greasy smoke which was forming a thick fog.

If that was meant to blind them, it had no effect upon the machine in which they sheltered. For that began again its ponderous advance onward, though all Thora could see was fog and raging flame. She expected to feel the heat of that through the shell of these walls, roasting them. For this was not just a barrier of fire, it spread quickly into a pool encompassing them.

But they felt no heat as on they went. Until before them, looming high as they so deliberately approached, was the bulk of the fortress. This was unlike any structure Thora had seen—more as if someone had found a mountain of stone and then set about rendering it into a citadel within walls nature herself had provided. There were slits which might be windows, but those were few, narrow, and placed well above ground level. While there was no sign of any door.

At last the crawler pulled to a halt facing a sullen reach of dark stone. Then into Thora's mind shot a sudden sharp command. She knew that came from Tarkin—even as her hands moved to obey and her voice repeated it aloud as if to better impress it upon her mind:

"Blue—yellow—white!"

Those were among the color pits on the board and she touched each in just that sequence. She saw that Makil was doing the same, trailed by Borkin a breath or so later.

There followed a brilliant lance of light, first rippling blue, then yellow, building to a near blinding white—shooting forth in three parts, to unite before those touched the stone. On the far edge of her screen Thora saw the coming of another such beam and believed that must spring from the second machine.

Now answered a sound, faint, far away. Still it hurt her head, seemed to pull at the muscles of her body as if it would take command of her, flesh and bones. A drummer? If so the crawler provided part protection against that other kind of attack.

Kort howled, pawing at his ears, his more sensitive hearing suffering the most. But, though human bodies twitched, and within Thora, at least, panic grew, they kept their fingers upon the buttons and the lance of light held true.

Held and ate. Beneath its touch rock crumbled, turning red, and then a sickly yellow—finally white. It fell in chunks and then actually melted into sluggish riverlets. The light opened a door where there had been none before.

So they broke the outer ring wall of the Dark fortress and moved on into an open way they had so uncovered. The lance of light shifted before them.

"Blue!" Again that order. Thora snatched away two fingers. The lance of light thinned to show them a pathway, rather than to destroy a barrier.

They trundled down a hall, between great pillars. Thora recognized this for a part of her vision. The thrumming of the drums became stronger. She must hold fast to the edge of the board with one hand in order to keep her seat, make sure her fingers were firmly in place.

The light fanned ahead, showing only emptiness. Where were the fighters Thora had confidently expected to see? That such had not shown also fed her growing fear. She could not believe that even these alien machines might so easily break the Dark defenses.

The drums—yes, the drums! Her body shook near beyond her ability to control it. That rhythm was stealing away her thoughts, blanking out her awareness. Could just *sound* defeat them so easily?

On went the crawler, not hurrying, continuing at the same steady speed it had kept on its journey across the land. Now that light lance reached and touched—held steady.

Drums—drummers—nine of them! Their drums ranged from one nearly as tall as the man who beat upon it, to another so small she might almost have cupped it in her hands, before which the drummer squatted in a hunkered position.

They did not seem startled when caught in the beam of the light. Instead their blind eyes stared straight at it. Their faces remained blank. They, themselves, might be machines fashioned in human form.

Thora waited for another order from Tarkin. Were they to turn upon these blind men that ravaging force of the combined lights? But there came no such command. The girl began to realize that the crawler, as powerful a weapon-transport as it might be—had never been intended for such a confrontation as this. There were other forces here, drawing battle onto another plane—one impervious to the machine. It seemed that the same thought had struck Makil, for he turned to Borkin, and then to Thora.

"This now becomes a matter of power—"

The girl cringed. She was certain that the carrier itself was a part protection against the force of the drums. To venture forth would put them at the mercy of that Dark weapon. Power—what she was so very little—nothing against this! Still she realized that there was no other answer—that they must now carry war to the enemy in what was indeed another way—armed only by what was open to those who walked the Path of Light.

Somehow Thora got to her feet. The blue lance had not disappeared when they raised their hands. It still illuminated the screen. Its intensity was also fed on the other side from the second crawler.

Makil, sword in hand, opened the door. Borkin crowded close behind him, wand at ready. Thora tore open her jerkin, not only to draw out her jewel, but to display the mark on her breast. She was the Lady's and in this war she would wear her mark proudly, even to death.

The drums were an agony. Even to move under that pounding beat which twisted and threatened them so was a torment. Still they stumbled and wavered to the front of the crawler, to face the drummers. None of those nine showed any awareness—they only continued to create that weapon of sound.

Thora saw both Makil's and Borkin's lips move, she was certain they were reciting some ritual. Now she raised the moon gem and breathed upon it, then spoke about its shape her own plea:

"I am the servant, Thou the Lady,
I am the hand to obey, the weapon to use,
   the body to serve—
I was born to Thy service, and by Thy will I
   live, to die at the time ordained.
Let now Thy great light come into me—I am
   a cup to be filled that I may do what is
   needful in this hour.
Blessed be Thy commands—let my ears hear
   them, my hands and feet to obey—
Blessed be ever the Will which moves me
   take me for Thy everlasting service—"

Strong was that ritual, one which only the Three-In-One might lawfully utter. But in this hour it was the only one to be used. If she erred in calling to her a power which was not hers, then death might well follow. Only there could be no faltering now—this was the life design.

Makil held high the Weapon of Lur. She could see the quivering of his body; he must be fighting hard against the drums. Borkin had his wand pointed outward. She drew on the last of her own strength and lowered the gem to the level of her heart.

From the tip of the wand began to uncoil a spiral which curved out and out. But from her own focus of force the radiance was not too defined—rather it spread as moonglow. The Lady's lamp hung not overhead, but lay in Thora's hand.

While the Weapon of Lur struck with its beam of clear light, and down that road sped the fighting sparks.

Those reached the drums, danced upon the taut skins, while the spiral fell, to encircle them, then began to tighten and draw in. A giant noose might so have been flung to catch drummers and instruments. The radiance engulfed all-dancing sparks, spiral, and the drummers.

There was a long moment when Thora feared failure—

Then the drums burst as they had in her vision. Those who had played them, tumbled to the pavement as if only the sound they had created were their real life—otherwise they were as the long-time dead.

Somewhere from high overhead, sounded a cry—of a rage so terrible that the very fury of it swayed Thora, already weakened by the drum power. She staggered, Makil caught her arm, steadied her. She was aware, in the blue light, of Tarkin erupting from the top of the crawler, taking a great leap to the second of the machines. It was toward that that they all now fled, pushing into the door held open for them, where Martan and Eban stood ready to haul them in. Thora saw Kort coming towards them. The hound's teeth were closed upon the hand of a man—one who stumbled and tottered, walked as blind-eyed as the drummers, one whom Borkin seized and bore with him into the shelter.

They dropped to the floor, strength drained out of them. Thora felt the shudder of the crawler coming to life. It was moving, where she could not have said.

When she could raise her head to look at the "windows" she saw that they were backing out of the citadel—emerging into the clear day. The machine lurched, shaking them from side to side. It was plain that it was being forced to the highest speed it could maintain.

She threw her arm about Kort, wondering dimly where he had found that man over whom Eban now bent. The dog was shaking violently but he did not even growl.

Now—the crawler was—were they about to return into the foul nest of the Dark?

Thora could have shouted that protest. Her attention was all for the "window." There lay the citadel, ugly under the sun, a blot on the whole world. She could see the ragged hole they had burned. Now she waited tensely for the enemy to issue forth from that—

There was a rumble; the very ground under the carrier moved. The solid earth might have been a wave across a pond. Then—the rise of rock before them quivered visibly. It moved—upward—outward—before collapsing upon itself into a huge, smoking pile of debris. The fortress had been reduced to rubble!

That crawler they had left behind—had it accomplished this without direction? Perhaps even that was possible by this strange other way of Power.

Thora was so drained she rested in a stupor of weariness, as she shared the cramped quarters during their journey back across the flatlands. What was put into her hands she ate, she drank when Tarkin or one of the others handed her a water bottle. Makil and Borkin looked to be in a hardly better state—Malkin hovering over her blood-brother, tending him. While Karn lay quiet but still living, a matter of concern for his fellows.

However when they reached the entrance to the storage place Thora shook off the daze which had held her so. She spoke to Tarkin first, for now she held the furred one of more importance than the valley men—in her own way.

"What will you do now—be what you say you were meant to be—a driver of these machines?"

"Not so. The flower cannot refold itself into a bud. We were seed planted, we grew, and we shall not return to what the Former Ones thought to make of us. These—" she looked to Martan, who as usual, was examining the machine with a very eager light in his eyes, "shall strive mightily to relearn the old secrets. I do not think they are wise, but such is their nature and they cannot deny it. We shall not aid them. We are free—what was once forgotten can be so again."

Thora gave a small sigh of relief. She had feared another answer—an awakening which was not of the Faith—perhaps a way which could lead to a new Darkness if they meddled too much with such soulless power.

"You are right, sister—" Tarkin's hand lay on hers. "Our answer is already there—" She nodded to the crawler. "You saw what its fellow did to the Dark Halls? This one, when we leave here, shall do the same for what has been hidden."

Thora watched Martan. "Will they let you?" she was doubtful.

"They shall have no choice. They have not the secrets we have. And such machines as these must not be loosed upon the world now," Tarkin said firmly and then continued:

"And you, sister, do you go to the valley?"

Thora smiled. "I think my answer to that you already know, Tarkin. Their life is not for me. I believe I was led here to serve the Lady—that in Her own way She has trained me as no other priestess has been fashioned before. Thus I remain in Her service, and *She* is not of the valley."

"That is so." Tarkin hesitated for a moment. "However, there may be perhaps one who will try to change your mind upon the matter."

Thora glanced at Makil who knelt by Karn, helping the rescued man to drink.

"He has Malkin—in a comradeship more complete, I believe, than any I can understand. No, I am a Chosen—and there must be more for me to do."

Tarkin's hands lay soft on her shoulders. "Slip away then, sister. But remember there remains a bond between us two—even though it is not sealed in blood. I, also, think that there is another way to walk. Go forth as the Maiden, for so you now are. Serve Her well—but watch often by your night fire, so shall I come—for I am also Chosen!"

With Kort as a silent shadow, her pack reclaimed, Thora did slip away before the fall of night. Saying no farewells, for those would be useless words. There remained a wall between which she had been wise enough to recognize. Makil was already claimed by custom. Nor did the Maiden take a mate. She was—free!

That word sang in her head as she ran, Kort by her side. The world opened before her. The Lady must have other plans. She would be a part of those before the final knot of the weaving was set and the pattern finished.

THE DRAGON REBORN

Sequel to *The Great Hunt*

Book Three of *The Wheel of Time*

by

Robert Jordan

Praise for *Eye of the World*

"A powerful vision of good and evil...fascinating people moving through a rich and interesting world." —Orson Scott Card

"Richly detailed...fully realized, complex adventure."
—*Library Journal*

"A combination of Robin Hood and Stephen King that is hard to resist...Jordan makes the reader care about these characters as though they were old friends." —*Milwaukee Sentinel*

Praise for *The Great Hunt*

"Jordan can spin as rich a world and as event-filled a tale as [Tolkien]...will not be easy to put down." —*ALA Booklist*

"Worth re-reading a time or two." —*Locus*

"This is good stuff...Splendidly characterized and cleverly plotted...The Great Hunt is a good book which will always be a good book. I shall certainly [line up] for the third volume."
—*Interzone*

The Dragon Reborn
coming in hardcover in August, 1991